ЯƎVⅡƧILVER

SUPERB WRITING
TO FIRE THE IMAGINATION

Louise Cooper writes: 'When I was little, one of my favourite games was to walk around the house holding a mirror angled towards the ceiling, and trying to navigate by the reflections I saw in it. I found the strange, reversed and upside-down world inside the glass endlessly fascinating, and often made up stories about the people and places that I might encounter there, if I could only reach inside.

I haven't played the mirror game for years, but the worlds of my books still have a lot in common with that long-ago fantasy. They and the mirror images are like borderlands between dreams and reality, and it's in those borderlands that I find inspiration when I write. I'll often look at some everyday scene or object or event, and think: If *this* or *that* aspect were changed, just a little, what new and strange tale might be told then? And so another story starts to take form.

The mirror sculpture that holds the key to Angel's adventures is very like those tracks of thought. Perhaps the worlds within it are a fantasy . . . but then again, who knows what new realities we might find, if we could only turn the key and open the door? The day I stop believing that it's possible will be the day I give up writing stories. And I don't think that's ever going to happen to me.'

*Other titles available from Hodder Children's Books:*

The Brugan
*Stephen Moore*

Daughter of Storms
The Dark Caller
Keepers of Light
Mirror Mirror 1: Breaking Through
Mirror Mirror 2: Running Free
*Louise Cooper*

Owl Light
Night People
Alien Dawn
*Maggie Pearson*

Power to Burn
*Anna Fienberg*

The Lammas Field
*Catherine Fisher*

The Takeaway Tales:
Aliens For Dinner
Yamabusters
Quirx: Welcome to Inner Space
Quirx: The Edge of the World
*Lesley Howarth*

The Law of the Wolf Tower
*Tanith Lee*

# MIRROR 3

# LOUISE COOPER

Hodder
Children's
Books

a division of Hodder Headline Limited

First published in 2001
by Hodder Children's Books

10 9 8 7 6 5 4 3 2 1

A Catalogue record for this book is available from
the British Library

ISBN 0 340 79654 5

Typeset by Avon Dataset Ltd, Bidford-on-Avon, Warks

Printed and bound in Great Britain by
Clays Ltd, St Ives plc

Hodder Children's Books
A Division of Hodder Headline
338 Euston Road
London NW1 3BH

This book is for yet more feline and canine friends. Purrs to . . . Tobermory, Crunchie, Toots, Lennier, Qatesh, Phoebe, Sparky, Elsie and Fluffy.
And tail-wags to . . . Daisy May, Berrin, Rio, Roxy, Sheba, Sasha, Gilbert, Bess and Glove.

# PROLOGUE

'If every moment of time contains an infinite number of possibilities,' Pye said, 'then anything and everything you can imagine must, logically, exist in one of those possibilities, mustn't it?'

Angel and Winter both stared at him, their faces studies in blank incomprehension.

Pye smiled. 'Oh, dear. You really haven't grasped it yet, have you? I think I'd better start with the absolute basics, and explain from there. You see, throughout all your travels, you have never visited different worlds, or even different times, but only different possibilities of *now*. Geographically speaking, you've never left Angel's city, or Winter's village, at all.

'It's a tricky concept to get to grips with, so perhaps it will help if I give you some examples from your own lives.' He twinkled at Angel. 'Take the day you stormed out of your fifteenth birthday party and stumbled on the secret of the mirror-door. What if you had *not* met the Marauders, and reached your home safely, to sulk in private? Or left the city altogether? If you had taken either of those courses, then none of your adventures would have happened. Likewise you, Winter. If Angel had not appeared through the waterfall and been hailed as a Spirit Childe, you would have gone on living in that Village of yours for the rest of an uneventful and – considering the epidemics – probably short life. In both your cases, the choice you *did* make was real, and the other choices that you did *not* make became "might-have-beens". So: each choice led to a *different* step, and then more *different* steps, until a whole string of "might-have-beens" was created.'

Pye gave them a few moments to absorb what he had said, then continued.

'You two young people are not from different times, but from different possibilities of *now*. Every time anyone makes any kind of a choice – and just consider how often that happens! – it leads to an event, which leads to other events, which in turn lead to the world being the way it is at the present moment.'

'But what *is* it at the present moment?' Winter asked. 'All the places we saw – which one is the *real* world?'

'They all are,' said Pye. 'Yours, mine, Angel's and all the others you visited. Every one is as real as the others, and every one is the result of one tiny choice!'

Such choices were a part of Pye's own story, too. As a young man he had been the most gifted student in his university year, but he was also a misfit, with some very unorthodox ideas. And at last the university elders lost patience with him.

'They made it clear that I was either to conform – at least until I was old enough to have "proper" knowledge and experience – or go away and be unconventional somewhere else, where I wouldn't be a nuisance to everyone. I was forced to make a *choice*.'

'And you did?' Angel prompted.

'I left the university; but not in the way my tutors expected.' Pye grinned. 'They wanted me to disappear, so I obliged them – by finding another reality, where I wouldn't be hampered by stuffy old men who couldn't see past the ends of their own noses.

'But,' he added, 'if I had agreed to conform instead, think what would have happened. I wouldn't have been free to experiment, so I wouldn't have invented the mirror-doors through which we have travelled. I wouldn't have found this reality and settled in it. And the three of us would never have met.'

Pye looked around at the glorious muddle of his workshop. 'I *like* misfits,' he said. 'And I've filled my new reality with them. Animals who were being exploited, plants that were being poisoned, objects which no one wanted any more . . . I've nurtured them, given them a new lease of life – guided them towards their own choices, if you like.'

'And now,' Winter ventured, 'Us . . .'

'Ah.' Pye studied them both thoughtfully. 'Yes . . . you *are* something of a problem. I didn't intend anyone else to find and use my doors. But there: no system is perfect, and mistakes do happen. However, I've been thinking about that, and I've come up with a solution.

'It's reasonable to suppose that if you discovered my little secret, others might do the same, That's a nuisance, because it means I will now have to patrol all the mirror doorways to stop intruders from meddling. I don't mind admitting that, at my age, it isn't a prospect I relish! I would *much* prefer to retire from the active side of my work, and find someone else to take over the chores of maintaining the doorways, doing the travelling and offering more fellow-misfits the chance of a better life.' His eyes gleamed at them, with a distinct hint of mischief. 'So it occurs to me that I need a young apprentice. Or possibly two . . .'

# ONE

The place looked rather like a park, except for the colours. In most parks, people don't paint the grass magenta, or tie bananas to oak trees, or decorate the bushes with glaringly clashing artificial flowers. But reality has many forms, and to the citizens who strolled along the paths or sat on conveniently placed seats in the pleasant shade of the trees, there was nothing at all bizarre about their surroundings.

The sun was beginning to slide down the sky, putting the time at roughly mid-afternoon. In the centre of a large circle of mosaic paving, a fountain played in the middle of a pool. The fountain contained a sculpture made of mirrors; light flashed and flickered from the mirrors' angles, creating dazzlingly dancing patterns. At the edge of the paving was a young woman on horseback. Her name was Suuu Beeen Aaat (usually), and at the moment she had startling orange hair; the horse (which was bored, and dozing) was basically dapple-grey, but one side of it had been painted chestnut. The paint, like the magenta of the grass, was flaking off in places.

No one took much notice of horse or rider. A few strollers, as they passed, said a polite 'Good morning!' or 'Goodnight!', then consulted the small minivids that everybody seemed to be holding and muttered a satisfied, 'Three (or 'six', or 'seventeen') to me!' before moving on.

Suuu Beeen Aaat ignored them all. She was much more interested in the fountain, for she believed that, soon, something was going to happen to it.

She had been waiting for about half an hour when her patience was rewarded. There was a sudden, violent flare of new light at the heart of the mirror sculpture; then a patch of air flickered and warped, and two people materialised into the middle of the pool. One of them –a woman some years older than Suuu – was dressed in a glittering interactive gown and waving an empty glass in one hand She uttered a fastidious squeak as water splashed her legs; her companion, who was also female but looked no more than ten years old, said something impatient and dragged her to the edge of the pool. The young one looked sharply at Suuu. Suuu looked back at her. Then she squinted at the sky, decided it was one of her truth times, and said,

'Ah. You again.'

The girl ignored that. 'Has anyone else been through since I last came?' she demanded.

Suuu shook her head. 'No.'

'Good.' The girl's companion was staring around and blinking a lot, and there was a fixed, artificial smile on her face, a smile that looked as if it had been practised a few thousand times in front of a mirror. At last she said, in an equally artificial and loud voice, 'This is . . . uhh . . . double-*A*. Totally *As* . . .'

Suuu Beeen Aaat looked at her with interest. 'Who's this one?' she asked.

'That's my business. She's famous; that's all I'm telling you.'

Suuu eyed the glass meaningfully. 'She's drunk, too, isn't she?'

The girl smiled a cold smile. 'I wouldn't know.' she said. 'Drunk, mad; whatever. Who cares?'

Suuu barked a short laugh. 'Mad, then. Most people are, once they've hung around with you for a while.' Then she smiled pleasantly. 'What part does she get?'

'I haven't decided,' the girl told her carelessly. 'Something quite good, probably. She's promising.'

'Mmm,' said Suuu non-committally. 'Oh, well. Good luck with her.' She frowned. 'I still wish you'd take me.'

The girl glowered back. 'I told you: you're not allowed. For one thing you're not famous, and for another you keep changing your mind. You wouldn't do as you're told, and you'd spoil everything, and that would make me cross. Very cross.' Her eyes narrowed, glinting. 'And you know what happens then.'

Suuu sniffed and said nothing. The girl watched her unpleasantly for a moment or two, then added, 'So you just keep a sharp lookout and tell me if there's anything I ought to know. Keep doing that, and I won't get cross. That's safer, isn't it – for everyone?'

Suuu shrugged again, though now with a distinct air of discomfort. 'All right,' she said reluctantly. 'Bye, then. Till next time.'

'Yes,' the girl agreed. 'Till next time.'

The older woman was staring at Suuu now, and the artificial smile was still there. 'I . . . uh . . . don't think we've *actually* been introduced,' she said. 'Are you from W?W?W? Or – no, don't tell me; I'm absolutely *telepathic*

7

about these things; it's another of my talents! – you're –
you're—'

'Be quiet!' the girl interrupted. She jerked the woman's
arm (they were attached to each other, Suuu saw now, by
a thin and faintly glowing cord) and pulled her back to
the sculpture in the middle of the pool. The older woman
started to protest, 'Darling, you can't just whisk me away
like this; it's so *rude*, and she might be someone *important*—'

But before she could get any further the brilliant light
flared again, and the two visitors were gone.

## TWO

'Hold her still . . . just a min longer . . .' The old man with the jaunty grey top-knot and one grey and one hazel eye glanced at his young apprentice and smiled encouragingly before concentrating on the bench again. 'One more little adjustment, and . . . *there*.' He stood back, and the smile became a beam. 'All right, Twinkle. You can wake up now.'

He unclipped two small connectors from one end of what looked like a heap of sparkling gold arti-fur. For a moment nothing happened. Then the heap twitched, wriggled, and resolved itself into the shape of a small, chubby cat that sprawled inelegantly on the bench-top with all four legs splayed. The cat opened wide silver-green eyes, blinked twice, and burped. Then in a high, cross voice it said,

'I'm *hungry!*'

'Ah.' The old man looked disappointed and a little abashed. 'No change there, then. I'm sorry, Angel. But I did warn you that it might not work.'

Angel Ashe suppressed a grin and scooped the little cat up in her arms. 'Don't worry, Pye,' she said. 'Even you can't perform miracles.'

Twinkle burped a second time. 'Fish?' she suggested hopefully.

'No way!' Angel protested. 'You sneaked four out of the

pool in the garden only yesterday, and don't try to pretend you didn't!'

Pye sighed. 'I'm afraid I must reluctantly conclude that Twinkle is a hopeless case,' he said. 'I've tried everything I know, and a few things I didn't know I knew, and every single one of them has failed. She's just plain greedy, and nothing in this reality, or any other, will cure her.'

Twinkle said huffily, 'I'm *not* greedy!' and wriggled to be put down. Angel set her on the floor, and she and Pye watched her wobble away in the direction of the workshop door. Twinkle was always a bit woozy after being anaesthetised for any length of time; something to do with her circuits having to realign themselves, Pye said, though Angel hadn't learned enough in only six months of apprenticeship to understand it properly. Reaching the door, the cat looked back reproachfully. 'Going to find Gregory,' she announced. '*He* gives me food!'

Her attempt at a dignified exit was spoiled by the fact that she walked smack into the wall twice before finally getting her sense of direction. Angel managed not to laugh as she disappeared. Twinkle's feelings were easily hurt – and, thanks to Pye, Twinkle really did *have* feelings now.

From the day she had received Twinkle as a present for her fifteenth birthday, Angel had never quite been able to think of her as a mere Therapet computer device. Twinkle had always had a personality and mind (admittedly eccentric and dippy) of her own. Pye, when he met her, had agreed. And with his genius he had set about a series of modifications that had transformed her from a bundle of wires and circuits and superconductors into . . . well,

Angel didn't pretend to comprehend exactly what Twinkle had become. Her body was still made up of wires and circuits and all the rest of it, but there was no possible doubt that she was *alive*, in a way she had never been before. She needed sleep now, like any living creature. She had moods, and the command 'Programme Terminate!' no longer put a stop to them. And, for the first time in her existence, she could eat. Tokyo, could she *eat*. It had taken Twinkle about point three of a sec to discover the joys of food, and now her whole life seemed dedicated to making up for all the meals she had missed before. She devoured anything and everything – she even liked the disgusting brown, smelly drink that Pye called Tee. Angel couldn't imagine where she put it all, but one thing was certain: if she could get away with it, Twinkle would simply go on eating until she exploded.

Angel looked around her at the wonderful chaos of the workshop, and smiled. Twinkle had changed enormously – but the change in Angel was just as great. The memory of her old existence in Zone Bohemia, Eurostate-8, had faded into the background; that fast, glittering world of computers and sponsors and jingles and instant pleasures seemed shallow and dream-like. Even Soho and Kim, her mother and father, were all but forgotten. She didn't miss them; and knew that they, in their turn, didn't truly miss her. This reality, Pye's reality, was her home now, and for the first time in her life she was *happy*.

She glanced out of the workshop's grubby window (Pye disapproved of too much cleaning; time, he said, had much better things to do with itself) and in the distance saw

Winter, her close friend and fellow-apprentice, driving cautiously across the vast, rambling garden in Pye's car. The car was an extraordinary contraption, nothing at all like the Autonet cars of her own world. It couldn't fly, it was open to the air, and it didn't propel itself automatically but had to be driven and guided and stopped and started by a human operator. Winter loved it, and was quickly learning how to handle it. Angel, though, had taken one look at the wheels, gears, brakes and other boggling paraphernalia that made it go, and decided that the sun would probably turn nova before she stood a chance of mastering it.

The fact that Winter *had* mastered it, and many more of Pye's assorted machines, had surprised Angel greatly. In Winter's reality, such things as cars were undreamed of; his primitive people couldn't even imagine basic sanitation, let alone engines, and Angel had confidently expected to surge parsecs ahead of him when their work with Pye began. Pye, though, had predicted that Winter would be a 'natural' with machinery, and he had been proved right.

Winter and the car were heading towards the workshop now, and as they approached there was a sudden painful roar from the engine, followed by a grinding squeal. Angel allowed herself to grin. Winter didn't often make a mistake, but when he did she couldn't help feeling a small twinge of pleasure. It wasn't something to be proud of, but she couldn't help it. Pye, now busy at another bench, looked round, saw her expression and raised the eyebrow above his grey eye.

'Shame on you, Angel!' he said. 'From someone who

can't even keep a Personabiwheel upright—'

She pulled a face. 'I am *trying* to learn it.'

'Indeed; and failing as dismally as I have with Twinkle's appetite! Speaking of which,' he straightened up. 'I'm hungry, too. Lunch, I think. Ring for Gregory, if you'll be so kind.'

Winter came in as they waited for Gregory to answer the bell. He had grown several centimetres in the past six months, and his white hair was cut short in a style that would have given Soho, Angel's fashion-crazed mother, a Traumatic Episode. His clothes would have doubled the Episode; baggy brown trousers with an equally shapeless jacket, all held together–with an assortment of metal fasteners and finished off with a pair of rough and heavy boots. Winter had made the garments himself, with Pye's help, and he was extremely proud of them. Angel thought they were unspeakable.

Gregory appeared. He was one of the strangest inhabitants in Pye's reality: a large, white, talking dog, with impeccable manners. Pye called him his 'Butler' (a weird concept that Angel hadn't quite got to grips with yet), and had rescued him from yet another now-possibility, where he and others like him were being exploited and ill-treated. Gregory was pushing the lunch trolley, on which was an assortment of steaming dishes, and Twinkle was trotting at his heels.

'I got some food,' she told Angel smugly.

Gregory looked as guilty as a dog's face can look. 'I'm sorry, madam,' he apologised. 'But she was *very* insistent. And it was only a morsel . . .'

13

Angel picked Twinkle up and plonked her on a battered couch. 'You're a little guts!' she told the cat. 'Now you can sit there and just watch us eat, and it serves you right.' She lifted the lid of a dish. 'Potatoes! Double-*A*! Pye, do you want some?'

Pye didn't answer. He was bending over his bench and didn't appear to have heard. 'Pye?' Angel repeated.

'Um? Oh – ah, yes, probably. What did you say?'

'Potatoes, Pye. Lunch. It's here.'

'Oh,' said Pye again. He sounded distracted. 'No . . . I don't think so. You two start without me. I just want to . . .'

His voice tailed off as he went back to what he was doing, and Angel frowned. There was something in his tone . . . he sounded concerned. Almost *worried*.

'Is something wrong?' she asked.

'What?' This time Pye did look up, but he hesitated before replying. 'No, no. Nothing wrong; nothing at all. Don't mind me; just carry on.'

She craned to see what he was doing, but all she could glimpse was a pile of papers with equations written all over them. Angel and equations weren't the best of friends, so that meant a great big zero. Hmm. *Something* was going on, and she wanted to know what it was. She'd bide her time, and get it out of Pye eventually.

She turned her attention to the food.

The computer control strip implanted in Angel's arm didn't work any more, simply because there were no computers here – or none that remotely resembled those of her old reality – for them to work with. So when she wanted to know the time, she had to look at a clock. Neither she nor Winter had ever seen clocks before coming to Pye's world, and Angel was still having trouble reading them; to her, they made no logical sense. But she *did* know that when both hands of the clock face were dead upright and together, it was either noon (she was trying not to call it Twelve-Hundred any more) or midnight. Now both hands were upright, and it was pitch dark outside; so midnight it must be. And she could still hear noises from the workshop.

The workshop took up half the ground floor of Pye's rambling house, and Angel's private quarters were directly above the heart of it. It wasn't like Pye to be working so late; normally he called a halt after the evening meal and fell asleep in his favourite battered chair for an hour or two before going to bed. Angel recalled his sudden distraction at lunchtime. He had assured her that nothing was wrong, but he had been in an odd mood all afternoon; vague and uncommunicative. There had to be a connection, and Angel wanted to know what was going on. Well then, the only thing to do was ask, wasn't it? She slid off her bed and made for the door.

Twinkle looked down from her current favourite sleeping place on top of the curtains and said, 'Where are you going?'

'To see Pye,' Angel told her. 'Coming?'

'Will he have any food?' Twinkle wanted to know.

'No way!'

'Pooey, then! Shan't come.' Twinkle went back to sleep, and Angel left the room. She paused outside Winter's door, wondering whether to invite him along. But what if she was wrong? Winter wouldn't take too kindly to being woken up for no good reason. Better to find out first, she thought.

The workshop door was ajar, and the room beyond was alive with flickering blue-white light. That could only mean Pye was experimenting with his mirror sculptures, the doorways he had invented and which allowed them to travel between realities. Was he creating a new doorway? Angel wondered. And if so, why was he being so secretive about it?

She edged into the room, shading her eyes as the light grew more intense. She could just make out Pye's rotund figure in the strobing chaos, and she spoke his name cautiously.

'Pye . . . ?'

'What?' Pye visibly jumped, then swung round. With light patterns dancing all over him his expression was hard to make out, but Angel thought that he looked alarmed for a moment before he masked it.

'Sorry,' she said, 'I didn't mean to startle you. But I could hear the noise, and it isn't like you to be working so late.'

Pye opened his mouth, closed it, hesitated, then opened it again.

'No,' he admitted. 'It isn't. I – ah—' Then his shoulders sagged. 'Oh, dear . . .' He reached behind him, pressed two switches and pulled a lever, and the flickering strobes slowed, faded and went out, leaving only a dim overhead light that turned everything to ghostly grey.

Now, Angel could see what Pye had been working on.

Behind him, only just visible in the gloom, was an elaborate structure of mirrors, metal arms and nozzles, standing twice her own height. This was the first and most vitally important of Pye's doors between realities; the master matrix from which all the others had sprung. It was far too valuable to stand unprotected in the workshop, and normally Pye kept it in an opaque shield-bubble. If he had uncovered it, something *must* be wrong.

Angel asked quietly, 'What is it, Pye? What's happened?'

Pye sighed. 'Oh, hell's bells . . . I didn't want to tell you, not until I could be sure. But now I have the unpleasant feeling that I *am* sure. So . . . I think you'd better come over here and look at this.'

He beckoned her to a side bench where a machine was clattering and muttering to itself as it slowly churned out an unending stream of paper. The paper was covered with graphs in twenty different colours and forty different patterns. It would be a long time before Angel would learn to make sense of the graphs, but one thing she *did* understand were the occasional sharp spikes, in red or purple, that stood out from the patterns like retro-freaks at a fad-radical party.

'Yes, I know,' she said, when Pye wordlessly pointed to the marks. 'When a doorway's used, a spike shows up on the record. We're always opening various doors, for maintenance.'

'Yes,' said Pye darkly. 'But these doors – here, and here, and here—' jabbing at spiked graph lines with a finger, 'are *not* on the maintenance schedule.'

Angel frowned. 'You mean, they opened without us touching them?'

'Exactly.'

She stared at the graphs again. 'Are you sure, Pye? There are so many doorways – couldn't you have made a mistake?'

'I could,' said Pye. 'So I checked. And then I double-checked. In fact I used four different checking methods, and they all tell me the same thing.' He rubbed a thumb over his chin, producing a faint rasping sound, and his brows gathered together in a frown as he turned to face Angel.

'It looks as though someone else has found out how to operate the doors between realities. And that *someone* has started using them.'

# THREE

It wasn't as if no one had ever discovered the doorways before. Angel had, albeit accidentally, when she fell into the mirror sculpture in the Cultural Enrichment sector of Zone Bohemia's Experience Mart all those months ago, and set off the chain of her adventures. But she and Winter had only used the doorways in an effort to get home. This, Pye said, was different. This time, someone was deliberately *meddling*. And he had a strong feeling that it could lead to big trouble.

He called Angel and Winter together for a conference early the next morning.

'I should have told you about it earlier,' he said as they all sat. 'But I didn't want to worry you.' He shrugged apologetically. 'It might just have been a glitch in the system.'

Winter shifted to make room for Twinkle, who was trying to climb on to his lap. 'But now you're sure it isn't?' he asked.

Pye nodded. 'I ran some more checks after I made Angel go back to bed.' He raised an eyebrow at Angel, 'and I'm afraid there's no possible doubt. So far, I've discovered seventeen of these spikes, and I wouldn't mind wagering that there are more that I haven't found yet. That poses a problem, because until I *have* found them all, there's no way of telling where and when they started.'

'So we don't know which reality this person comes from?' said Angel.

'Exactly. Mind you, even if we did know, it probably wouldn't do us a lot of good, because I very much doubt that our unknown troublemaker intends to stay in his – or her – own world. If they did, they wouldn't be using the doorways in the first place, would they?'

'That makes sense,' Winter agreed. 'So what *can* we do?'

'What about shutting down all the doorways?' Angel suggested. 'That'd glitch their programme.'

'It would; but we'd have to visit each reality in turn and dismantle every single mirror sculpture.' Pye smiled wryly. 'Have you any idea how long that would take?'

She looked crestfallen. 'Ah. Right. I see what you mean.'

'So,' Pye continued, 'unless either of you has a better idea, I think we must concentrate our efforts on tracking down every use of the doorways, and try to find a pattern to them. If we can, then it should be a relatively simple matter to anticipate our friend's next move and set a trap to catch him or her.'

Winter let out his breath in a long whistle. 'That could take nearly as long as shutting down all the doorways!'

'Not quite; though I take your point. However, I see no other practical choice.' Pye paused, waiting for any more suggestions. Twinkle looked up and said, 'Tee and crumpets!' in a firm voice, but that was hardly helpful, and Angel's and Winter's faces were blank.

'Right,' said Pye, heaving himself to his feet. 'Then I think we'd better begin.'

20

★ ★ ★

Within a few days, they were beginning to realise just how big the trouble was.

Pye had found no less than thirty-eight spikes on the graph records. They stretched back over several weeks, and more were being added every day. Frustratingly, there was no pattern to them at all as far as anyone could see, and a dozen different calculating machines from a dozen different realities couldn't make head or tail of the information Pye fed them.

Pye paid visits to some of the realities whose doors had been opened, but found no clues – or so he thought at first. But after a while, something *did* grab his attention.

He called Angel and Winter to a crack-of-dawn meeting. The three of them had been conferring regularly every day, but this hour was so out of the ordinary that they knew something significant must have happened.

Pye didn't waste time. 'It may be meaningless,' he told them, 'but my bones tell me that it isn't. It's happened . . . let's see . . .' he consulted a hand-held gadget that beeped and whirred back at him . . . six times now, and in my view that is pushing coincidence too far.' A pause. 'People are *disappearing*.'

'What?' Angel swallowed a sleepy yawn and her eyes widened. 'From those realities, you mean?'

'Yes. In every case it's some prominent person – a celeb, as they say in your world. That's how I know, you see; vanishing celebs mean an enormous hoo-hah, and I walked straight into the middle of the uproar on my visits. In each case, the disappearance seems to have happened at the same time that a new spike appeared on my graphs.'

Winter whistled. 'You're right: that's no coincidence!'

'Quite so. Unfortunately, it doesn't really help our investigations, as there's no other obvious connection between the disappearances; in fact the choice of celeb seems to be as random as the spikes themselves.' He frowned. 'But it gives a new and very unpleasant dimension to this whole affair. We've been telling ourselves that, if we are vigilant and patient, a pattern will eventually emerge. Now though, I don't think we can afford to wait for that to happen. This has gone beyond mere meddling. It's becoming downright dangerous.'

'But what can we do?' Angel asked.

Pye's frown intensified. 'Work, work, work,' he stated flatly. 'Check and double-check every scrap of data, explore and re-explore every possible avenue, however unlikely it might seem. And overlook *nothing*. This person must be found. And they must be *stopped*.'

For three days it looked as if they were going to get nowhere. Then, shortly before midnight of the third day, there was a development.

Winter and Pye were at opposite ends of the workshop, concentrating on separate tasks. Angel was in bed; she had fallen asleep twice at her work this evening and hadn't had the energy to make even a token protest when Pye sternly told her that enough was enough. Gregory had come in a few minutes ago, but no one had noticed him and the Tee on his inevitable trolley still stood untouched. Silence had reigned for what seemed like an age, until at last Winter straightened up from his bench.

'Pye, when you re-set the differential monitor after an abreaction, should you re-calibrate the indicator first or afterwards?'

Pye didn't respond. Winter looked round – but Pye wasn't there. 'Pye?' He hurried to where the old man had been working.

A mirror sculpture was set up beside Pye's bench; not the matrix but simply one of the working doorways, and as Winter approached, light suddenly flared in the glass. There was a faint, high-pitched hum that lasted only a sec or two, then Pye materialised from the sculpture. He stumbled out on to the workshop floor, blinked, saw Winter and said, 'Oh, hell's bells . . .'

Winter had been about to ask his question again, but Pye's words, and the horrified expression on his face, stopped him in his tracks. 'What's wrong?' he asked.

Pye didn't answer the question; he only replied, 'You'd better wake Angel. Immediately.'

'Why?' The fear swelled. 'What's happened?'

Pye shut his eyes and pressed the fingertips of one hand to his forehead. 'Another celeb has disappeared,' he said. 'But this time there's a personal connection with us.' He looked haggardly at Winter. 'The new victim is from Angel's reality. It's Soho – her mother.'

It was crazy, Angel thought as she stood in the workshop. Both Winter and Pye had expected her to cry, and if she thought about it logically, she would have expected it of herself. Her Prime Parent had suddenly and inexplicably vanished, and could be in desperate danger or even dead by now. Surely she *should* cry? In fact she ought to be having a full Traumatic Episode, in best Soho style. It was the sort of thing people *did*. Instead, though, as Winter and Pye looked worriedly on, and Twinkle (who hadn't quite grasped yet what was going on) ran round her in circles saying, 'Don't worry, Angel, don't worry, Angel!', all she wanted to do was laugh. It was the thought of Soho being classed as a celeb that did it. She wasn't anything of the kind; not in her own right, anyway. She'd only become famous because Angel had been famous; and Angel had only been famous because she'd disappeared from her world and then miraculously returned. But Soho was never one to miss an opportunity, so when Angel left for good she must have used her wiles to stay in the limelight. It was just *typical*.

Winter said uneasily, 'Angel . . . are you all right?'

She turned her head quickly to look at him. 'Of course I am.'

Winter glanced at Pye. 'She might be in shock—'

'Don't be such a frog, I'm double-A!' Angel said scornfully. 'It's just . . . well . . .' *Oh, flackers, what's happened to Soho?* Suddenly the full realisation of the situation hit her. She put her knuckles in her in her mouth and bit them.

'Now, now; there, there,' Pye soothed. 'It's quite understandable, my dear Angel; she's still your mother, after all. Of course you're concerned.'

'It's not concern, exactly, it's . . . oh, hell's bells . . .' Angel used Pye's expression because at this moment it seemed horribly apt.

'Of course, and I understand. So if you want to help her—'

'I do!' said Angel helplessly.

'Good. You can. By coming with me to your reality.'

She stared at him. 'What?'

Pye's grey eye had an eager glint in it, while the hazel one looked resolute and almost cold. 'Have you ever heard the saying about clouds and silver linings? No? Well, in effect it means that there is a positive side to every misfortune. Utter twaddle for the most part; but in this case it might just be true. Soho's disappearance is the cloud, but your connection with her is the silver lining. In fact, the lining might prove to be solid gold.'

'I don't understand.'

'You will.' Pye was looking at her left forearm, where the control strip Soho had given her for her fifteenth birthday was implanted. The strip gave Angel a personal link to computer and communications networks in her own reality; here, of course, it was completely useless. But there was an eager undercurrent in Pye's voice. He met her gaze, smiled, and touched a finger to one side of his nose in a conspiratorial gesture.

'I'll explain when we get there. For now, I suggest you go and put on something suitable for a short visit home.'

At a glance, they looked just any other pair of media execs. Some black-and-white drapes and a quick face-make with chalk and oil from the workshop had transformed Angel into someone making a definite Fashion Statement, while Pye wore a long robe with a cowl that hid his face and a fake hol-glitter halo (some of the newsdrones were heavily into dressing up as 'Seekers After Truth'). They both carried impressive-looking devices – or gizmos, Pye called them – that didn't do anything but could pass well enough for the latest in soundpix recorders.

Angel's heart was thumping as she and Pye stood in front of the mirror sculpture. She didn't know which was worse: the thought of what might have happened to Soho, or the prospect of stepping back into her old reality. They both made her feel sick with nerves. Pye, understanding, squeezed her hand and flicked her a reassuring smile. Then Winter said, 'Ready', and there was a hum, a flare of light—

'No, no, nonoNO! Darling, I said *there*, under the sponsor's logo! And look *agonised*, sweetie, just as if it was your own Prime Parent who had disappeared!'

'Come on, hons, take no notice of the others – Infax viewers want to see *real tears*, so cry-cry-*cry!*'

'Where in Tokyo has that flackering security leader *gone?* Do these spiders think we've got mins to waste?'

Soho's mirror sculpture, which had once been Angel's, was displayed on a plinth in one corner of an enormous room that was so fashionable that, as Soho herself might have put it, it wasn't merely As but absolutely *pre*-As. The room was heaving with people, who were all far too excited to notice Angel and Pye emerging from the sculpture. Newsdrones, media execs, celeb-chasers, security operatives; there were even a few red Vigilant uniforms in the jostling, babbling crowd. Whirligigs zoomed in all directions, broadcasting messages that weren't aimed at anyone but just added to the general uproar. A wave of heat and noise hit the newcomers, advertising holos played across the walls and ceiling, and it took Angel several secs to realise that this must be Soho's new condo, the one she'd been about to move to when Angel finally fled for good to Pye's world.

As they stepped off the plinth someone collided with them, mouthed, 'Apols, yuh?' and charged on through the chaos. Music blared suddenly out of invisible speakers as the holos on the walls changed to pix of Soho's face. There was a mass gasp, right on cue, and someone yelled blissfully, 'Double-*A!* Let's hear it again, people! Where *is* Soho Ashe?'

Pye didn't waste any time. 'Follow me!' he bawled in Angel's ear above the background din. 'And if anyone speaks to you, ignore 'em!'

They fought their way to and through the nearest aperture. The hall outside was bulging with braying people, but they managed to find a corner where they could just about hear each other and wouldn't be barged too often.

'Right,' said Pye. 'Now activate your arm strip.'

Angel looked at him blankly. 'Uh?'

He grinned. 'Your Personalink number. It's connected to Soho's, isn't it?'

Everyone was assigned a Personalink at birth, and anyone under the age of seventeen had their number sub-routed through their Prime Parent's ID. The idea – as Angel had discovered, more than once, to her cost – was to let the Prime Parent keep track of their child *and* the

27

comms bills that were being run up. Now though, Pye had another use for the link.

'It's a long shot,' he said, 'but it's just possible that we might be able to use your Personalink to find out where Soho has gone. She could track you through her implant, so if I can reverse the circuit . . .'

'Then maybe we can track her!' Angel's eyes lit eagerly. 'Double-*A!* What do we do?'

'First, see if you can communicate with her. Switch on, switch on!' Pye flapped his hands, as excited as she.

Angel raised her arm and touched a code into the strip. 'Input,' she said. 'Personalink communications.'

A green light blinked in the strip and a tinny voice said, 'Acknowledged, Angel Ashe.'

'Direct comm with Soho Ashe; priority-A.'

There was a pause. A long pause. More lights came on and skittered over the strip in mad patterns. Then finally: 'No can do, Angel Ashe. Soho Ashe is out of range.'

Angel said a word under her breath, but Pye urged, 'See how far the computer can follow her.'

She nodded. 'Input: info enquiry, location mode. Where *is* Soho?'

Another lengthy pause, then the voice replied, 'Theoretical location: Condo Silver-Two, Zone Celeb, Birmingham, Eurostate-8. Actual location unknown.' More lights chased each other. 'Track?'

'Track.' Angel's heart rate was speeding up again.

'Hold . . . inputting . . .' Several bleeps followed. 'Total track not possible. Partial track result as follows: Seven-double-zero-stroke-X, phasal shift at point-oh-five, pre-set channel four-one. Results inconclusive.'

'*What?*' Angel was boggled, and her temper rose. 'You stupid frogging thing, what sort of drivel are you—'

'No, Angel, wait!' Pye interrupted. He had produced a small hand-pad and stylus. 'Tell it to repeat what it just said.'

Angel did. The list of jargon meant no more to her than it had done the first time, but Pye was exultant. 'Got it! Marvellous! With this data, I should be able to—'

The rest of his words were eclipsed by a shrieking siren, and another Whirligig came hurtling from the main room. It shuddered to a stop, and everyone looked up as it hovered and bounced above their heads.

'INFO FLASH! INFO FLASH!' the 'gig blared. 'DATA INDICATOR: RUMOUR LEVEL NINE – SOHO ASHE'S DAUGHTER ANGEL ASHE, IN PERSON, IS SOMEWHERE IN THIS CONDO!'

Under the chalk-and-oil make, Angel's face blanched. 'Oh, Tokyo – someone's recognised me!'

'More likely your control strip triggered off an alert,' Pye told her. 'We'd better make ourselves scarce.'

He started to shepherd her back towards the aperture. The 'gig was now spinning in circles, announcing, 'BOUNTY BIDS: INFAX OFFERS TWO THOUSAND CREDS AND PRIME-TIME PERSONAL EXPOSURE FOR POSITIVE ID OF ANGEL ASHE!' A blistering beep. 'THE TERRAVENTURE NETWORK OFFERS TWO THOUSAND FIVE HUNDRED CREDS, ONE

YEAR'S FREE CHANNELSURF *AND* A MINOR ROLE IN A FORTHCOMING EPISODE OF *MEGATERROR!* THE HAMAMOTO-EMPATHY CORPORATION PLEDGES—'

Angel and Pye scurried through the aperture. But another 'gig was there before them, blasting the same message at the crowd in the main room. Hamamoto-Empathy were apparently leading the bidding so far, and the newsdrones were wildly excited. Several of them were grabbing randomly at anyone they didn't know, in case they should turn out to be Angel Ashe, and arguments started to flare. Pye towed Angel between two execs from W?W?W? and the Heartbreak Hell Channel (who were pulling at the arms of a bewildered young proto-celeb and squabbling hotly over Who Saw Her First) and they scrambled on to the plinth where Soho's sculpture stood. Angel saw Pye flick a sharp glance over the mirrors and thought he was going to say or do something. But one or two drones were starting to look at them, and he thought better of it.

'Ready?' He grabbed Angel's arm. 'Go!'

Noise, light. This time people did notice, because they were all on the lookout now. However, all anyone actually saw was two figures on the plinth, framed in a momentary bright flare. Then the light vanished and the two figures were no longer there.

A senior exec from W?W?W? stared at the spot where Angel and Pye had been, and said to her assistant, 'Did you *see* that? *Screaming!*'

'A-*hu*,' the assistant agreed, blinking long purple

eyelashes. 'Double-now holo, yuh? Uh . . . who were the performers?'

The exec shrugged. 'Newbies, darling. Must be, or I'd have clicked with them. Maybe we'll target later; but not now.' She glared round the room like a predatory animal. 'Never mind Soho going missing – Angel Ashe coming back is *mega*-news! If she has, I want the exclusive, and I want it *now*. So get looking, sweetie – and if you miss a *milliatom* of a clue you'll be programming Autonet routes for a living tomorrow morning. Connect?'

She stalked off in a flurry of interactive draperies, leaving the assistant staring resentfully after her and wondering if Infax would be interested in another kind of exclusive altogether.

# FOUR

Back in the workshop Winter was brimming with questions, but neither Pye nor Angel was in a mood to answer them. Pye headed straight for his cluttered bench, where he soon had a motley assortment of machines clicking and chugging and humming, while Angel felt too shaken up by the visit to her old home to want to talk. So an awkward silence fell, broken only by the background muttering of the machines, until after perhaps half an hour Pye punched the air with a clenched fist and shouted exultantly, 'Got it!'

They hurried to the bench. A new machine was buzzing and blinking there: one of Pye's latest inventions, and on the surface nothing more spectacular than a small grey box with rows of lights on it. Angel and Winter hadn't the least idea what it did or how it did it, but it seemed that it had given Pye what he wanted. A faint wisp of smoke was rising from the back of the machine, suggesting that something inside it had overloaded. And the graph recorder, to which it was attached by a long piece of wire, had churned out a whole new ream of paper.

'There!' Pye said, jabbing a finger at the graph. There were two spikes at the spot he indicated, and a wavy blue line extended from one spike and on down the length of the paper.

Angel's eyes lit eagerly. 'Is that Soho's trace?' she asked.

'It most certainly is. And this spike here . . .' Pye swept a few metres of paper aside and pounced on another section, '. . . shows me where she went!' Snatching up another, smaller gizmo from the bench, he plugged it into the graph recorder and punched buttons. 'This will identify the exact doorway, and then we can . . .'

His voice tailed off as a string of figures appeared on the gizmo's readout, and he frowned very deeply.

'What is it?' Angel asked.

'I don't believe it . . .' Pye was speaking to himself rather than answering her. 'This is quite *ludicrous* . . .'

'What?' she repeated more sharply. 'Do you know which doorway it is?'

'Oh, yes.' Pye looked up at last. 'But I'm very surprised. In fact, I'm shocked and disappointed.' He shook his head. 'For all their faults, I really wouldn't have thought they would get involved in such a thing . . .'

'*Who* wouldn't get involved?' Angel was getting close to screaming point.

'What?' Pye blinked. 'Oh, didn't I say? Well, there's no point wasting time with words: better if we all travel there, right now, and have this out.'

Pocketing the small gizmo, he bustled away towards the matrix sculpture, then glanced back at them. 'Come along, come along! Or I'll have to go without you.'

Angel and Winter exchanged a baffled glance, then Winter shrugged. 'Who are we to argue?' he said.

They hurried after Pye. Twinkle, who had been dozing on top of a teetering pile of books, opened one eye and watched as they positioned themselves in front of the sculpture. Light began to flicker, but Twinkle had seen it all before and wasn't impressed. Vaguely wondering where her friends were going, and if they would bring her back anything interesting to eat, she yawned, shut the eye and went back to sleep as Pye, Angel and Winter vanished.

Winter looked around him and said, 'We've been here before.'

Angel remembered all too well. An elaborate fountain in a circular pool, set in a park that had to be one of the most bizarre places ever created. It had all the expected park ingredients: well-tended trees and bushes, neat paved paths, flowerbeds and seats. But an assortment of unlikely objects – everything from garish fake flowers to bananas and pineapples – were tied to the bushes' branches with pieces of string, and the grass was painted magenta. Or most of it was, Angel corrected herself as she took it all in: for there were patches of brilliant blue or yellow here and there, as if someone had grown bored with the magenta and was haphazardly experimenting with new colours.

She looked at Pye and said, 'Oh, Tokyo – you think our troublemaker is from *this* reality?'

Pye nodded glumly. 'I'm afraid so. And the inhabitants' obsession with lies and silly games is going to make our task very hard indeed.'

Her heart sank as she remembered the citizens of this world, whom she and Winter had encountered on their first visit. To say they were mad was putting it mildly; almost no one ever told the truth, and everyone seemed to revel in creating confusion wherever they went.

'There's only one hope,' Pye continued. 'It's a slender one, because she might genuinely know nothing about this. But if we can find an old acquaintance of mine – ah!'

Bang on cue, a horse appeared round a clump of small trees that sported fake stars on their boughs. Half of the horse was a natural dapple-grey; the other half had been painted green. On its back, looking totally relaxed and smiling at them, was a woman with matching green hair.

The horse reached them, stopped, and the woman's smile widened. 'Goodnight,' she greeted them pleasantly.

'Blast!' said Pye. 'It isn't one of her truth times.' He eyed the woman sternly. 'Good *morning*, Suuu Beeen Aaat. Don't try to tell me that it's anything else, and don't try to pretend you don't know me, because *I* know you're lying!'

'That's the idea.' Suuu Beeen Aaat beamed, then scrutinised Pye's companions. 'Who are they?'

'You know perfectly well, because you've met them before.'

'No, I haven't.'

Pye sighed. 'We could waste hours with this game,' he told Angel and Winter. 'I think I'll have to try a few little tricks . . .' Turning back to Suuu he said, 'I want you to answer some questions.'

'Not a chance,' said Suuu.

'That means yes, so I suppose it's a start. Right. Has anyone gone or come through the mirror doorway since I was last here?'

'No.'

'They have. Good. How many times?'

'Once.'

'More than once, then.'

'This could take forever!' Angel hissed.

Pye glowered at her. 'If you've got a better suggestion—'

'Well, no . . .'

'Then, to use a phrase from your world, kindly shut down your programme.' Angel flushed and Pye turned back to Suuu. 'Where was I? Ah, yes. This person you've never seen, who didn't come or go through the sculpture. Did they travel alone?'

'Absolutely,' said Suuu.

'Aha!' Triumph glinted in Pye's eyes. 'So it seems likely that the abductees weren't snatched away from a distance but were accompanied by our mysterious friend in person. I think we're starting to get somewhere, but I must phrase my questions very carefully if we're going to winkle any more out of her.' He cleared his throat. 'Now, Suuu—'

'Never heard of her,' said Suuu cheerfully.

Pye ignored that. 'These two travellers—'

'There weren't two,' she interrupted. 'There were . . . oh, sixteen of them. And they weren't really here.'

Pye nudged Angel in the ribs. 'You hear that?' he said under his breath. 'The fact that she actively denies there were two means there must have been exactly *two*, no more and no less!'

'But how does that help?' Angel hissed back.

'Process of elimination, my dear girl. Tedious, but it works, eventually. Right: next question.' He raised his voice again. 'This person. The one who wasn't here and didn't go through the sculpture. You know who it is, of course?'

He expected Suuu to grin and say smugly that of course she didn't, but to his dismay her face fell.

'Bother!' she said. 'Yes, I know exactly who it is. We've been friends for . . . oh, *centuries*. So that's seven points to you.' Out of a pocket came a hand-held minivid, and she keyed something into it. 'Bother!' she repeated.

'Oh.' Pye's face had fallen, too. 'I hadn't bargained for this.'

'You mean, she doesn't know them?' asked Angel.

He shook his head. 'She hasn't a clue, or she wouldn't have said "exactly". Mmm. That *is* unfortunate.'

He waded into the pool, took the small device he'd brought out of his pocket and aimed it at the mirror sculpture. The device bleeped and two red lights and one green appeared and started to chase each other round in circles.

Suuu watched with great interest. 'What a boring toy,' she said. 'You can't use *that* to find out where the people who weren't here didn't go.' Pye only grunted, and she looked faintly piqued. 'They invited me along, of course. Begged me, in fact. But I said no. I wouldn't go if they paid me. I . . .' She stopped, and her expression changed. '*Ow*! My head's hurting . . . oh, I *hate* these moments; they're so—' A shiver ran through her. 'No, I don't hate them! I don't; I—*oooh* . . .'

Rocking back in the saddle she clutched her skull, shutting her eyes tightly and grimacing. The green-and-grey horse tossed its head and whinnied nervously; it started to back away but bumped into a seat, which made it kick out in surprise.

'Hey!' Suuu snapped out of her fit, or whatever it was, and grabbed the reins, hauling the horse round. 'Idiotic animal, you'll have me tipsy-over in a minute! *Whoo!*' She shook her head, making the green hair fly out in a violent halo, then heaved a deep, relieved breath and looked at Angel and Winter as if seeing them for the first time. 'Well, good morning!' she said brightly. 'I've met you before, haven't I? You came through the sculpture some time back, and you – ah!' She had seen Pye. 'This *explains* it.' And, more loudly, 'Hello, Pye. I might have known you'd be involved.'

Pye swung round with a look of profound relief. 'Suuu. Praise be to whatever powers are listening, you're back to your truth time!'

'Am I?' Suuu thought about it for a moment or two. 'Oh, yes; so I am. Sorry about that. Have you been hanging around for long?'

'It could have been worse. I need your help, Suuu.' Pye splashed out of the pool and approached her. 'It's about the people who have been using the doorway.'

Suuu said uneasily, 'Ah . . .'

'I need to know as much as you can possibly tell me,' Pye went on, not noticing the abrupt change. 'I realise that the troublemaker isn't personally known to you, but—'

Suuu held up a hand. 'Wait, Pye, wait.'

'What do you mean, wait? I want some answers, and I haven't got time to waste on games!'

'I'm not playing games,' said Suuu. 'But I *have* got a problem.'

Pye hesitated. 'What kind of a problem?'

She was looking extremely uncomfortable by this time. 'Look, Pye, you know me. When it's not my truth time, I always tell lies. But when it *is* my truth time, I don't lie. In fact, I can't; something inside stops me. If you make me answer your questions, everything I say will be true.'

'Indeed,' Pye agreed. 'So—'

'So that's where the problem is. I don't want to answer, Pye. I don't want to tell you what I know about . . . *them*.'

'Why ever not?'

'Because . . .' Suuu paused, then suddenly hung her head. 'Because of what might happen to me if I do.' Her head came up again and she added with a nervous, almost childlike defiance, 'Because I'm *scared*.'

Pye stared at her, nonplussed. 'Scared . . .? Suuu, this is nonsensical! In all the years I've known you, I've never once seen you afraid of anything!'

'Maybe that's because there wasn't anything to be afraid of,' said Suuu. 'But there is now.' She swept a quick, furtive look around her, as if half-expecting to see spies behind every bush, then her voice dropped to a whisper. 'If I tell, then . . . someone . . . will get *cross*. I saw, once, what happens when they get *cross*. And I don't want to see it again! So don't ask me anything, Pye. Just *don't*!'

She jerked at the horse's reins, bringing its head round, and drove her heels into its flanks. The suddenness of it took them all by surprise, and no one had time to protest or make any move at all before the horse had taken off at a standing gallop and was charging away down one of the paths.

'Suuu Beeen Aaat!' Pye shouted after her. 'Suuu! Come back!'

But Suuu ignored him, and within a few more seconds she was out of sight.

Pye, Angel and Winter all stared at each other as the sound of hooves faded away. None of them spoke for some while, and the silence was becoming very tense when at last Winter ventured to break it.

He said slowly, 'I don't think I like this . . .'

'And I think you're very wise not to,' Pye told him. 'For whatever else Suuu Beeen Aaat may be, she is *not* a coward.'

'She really was scared,' Angel said.

'She was. And when I ran my trackscanner over the sculpture in the pool, I discovered something else that's dislikeable.' He held up the small device. 'This shows me the latest incoming and outgoing paths that have been used through the mirrors. The readout clearly shows an incoming path from my workshop, which is just as it should be. However, unless something is wrong with the device – which I very much doubt – the *outgoing* trace doesn't lead to any known doorway.'

Angel stared at him in dawning horror. 'You mean that Soho was whisked away to – to *nothing*?'

Pye shook his head. 'No, my dear,' he said hollowly. 'I don't mean that at all. I mean that the doorway that was used isn't known to *me*. In other words, I didn't build it.' He hunched his shoulders and fixed his gaze on the fountain, though Angel had the impression that he wasn't truly seeing it.

'For someone to discover how the reality doors work is one matter,' he added. 'It's happened before and I don't doubt it will happen again; my security systems are far from infallible. But this meddler is different. This meddler not only knows how to use the doors, they have also discovered how to *make* them. I know how much skill that takes. I also know the strength of the temptation it gives rise to. The temptation of *power*. It's extremely hard to resist. So . . .' He switched the trackscanner off, and the circling lights died. 'I'm beginning to understand why our good friend Suuu is afraid. In fact . . . I'm more than a little afraid myself. And I think I have good reason.'

# FIVE

Though he wasn't at all happy about the plan, Pye had to admit that it made sense. Quite simply, the only way to learn anything about the new reality doorway was to go through it and see what lay on the other side. And it was only logical that Angel and Winter should be the ones to make the jump. As Winter pointed out, someone had to stay in the workshop to monitor what was happening, and only Pye was capable of doing that. At last, reluctantly, Pye gave way.

'But you must take the greatest care,' He warned them. 'Any number of dangers could be waiting for you – remember the radioactive world that I snatched you out of just in time?' He saw them both shiver, and nodded, satisfied that he'd made his point. 'So at the *slightest* sign of trouble, you come back here without any delay. Is that understood?'

It was, and Angel in particular took notice of the warning. Though she didn't say so to Pye or Winter, she felt distinctly uneasy at the prospect of visiting a reality that none of them knew the first thing about. It was silly, but her biggest fear wasn't of poisoned atmospheres, or mad people, or any of the obvious hazards. What unnerved her was the thought that she might step into a slightly different version of Zone Bohemia (or Zone Celeb, where

Soho's sculpture was now) and come face to face with another Angel Ashe. It had happened once and had been one of the most horrible experiences of her entire life; and she was not at all anxious to repeat it.

The existence of many other, equally real Angels in many other versions of now was still one of the hardest things of all for her to come to terms with. There were, of course, just as many realities in which she *didn't* exist, because the chain of events there had been so different that neither she nor any of her ancestors had ever been born. Winter's world (as far as she knew) was one, as was Suuu Beeen Aaat's world of liars and, thankfully, the terrifying 'nows' that she and Winter had encountered during their early adventures. But here she was to be faced with a reality that was new even to Pye. Did Angel Ashe exist in that world? Or had she never been thought of? Or – the worst prospect of all – had she existed, but died of some disease, or in a gruesome accident, or even in a cataclysmic war?

She was preoccupied with her worries and speculations as she and Winter made their preparations. Pye had given them some new equipment to carry with them; an assortment of devices that included scanners, recorders, alarms and a host of other features. Angel tried to listen as Pye explained what everything did and how it worked, but she knew she wasn't taking any of it in. She could only hope that Winter was absorbing Pye's instructions and would know what to do if the need arose.

Their departure was set for mid-morning on the following day. Angel was too nervous to face breakfast, but Winter ate heartily. So did Twinkle, who, to everyone's surprise, had announced firmly that she wanted to go, too.

'There might be fun,' she said. 'I *like* fun. Learn some new games!'

'I think it's a good idea,' Pye agreed. 'You never know when some of her abilities might come in useful.' He looked at Twinkle sternly. 'But I suggest you put her on a lead.'

So at the appointed time the three of them stood in front of the matrix sculpture while Pye, consulting the records and notes he had made, began his careful adjustment of the mirrors. Twinkle was attached to Angel by a sparkling and immensely strong gold lead that was clipped to a harness around her ample middle. She didn't like it, but it was a case of putting up with it or staying behind, so she grumpily gave in, though she kept screwing her head round and trying to bite the harness when she thought no one was looking.

At last Pye said, 'Ready!' Then he repeated his last-minute instructions and warnings, and wished them good luck. Angel's heart was pumping madly; she took a deep breath, glanced at Winter, who smiled reassuringly. 'Into the unknown,' he said. 'We're intrepid explorers!'

She wished he hadn't said that, and started to open her mouth to say, 'I don't want to go'. But it was too late. Light was flaring in the depths of the mirrors; reflections danced and shimmered in a hundred different images of her own face. Impulsively she scooped Twinkle into her arms – then there was noise, and an explosion of brilliance, and—

They stumbled out of the doorway and were confronted by a blare of dazzling pink.

Angel and Winter both recoiled from the shock of the colour, and Twinkle squeaked with astonishment. The dazzling pink was a wall, three times Angel's height, that completely surrounded them in a circle some ten metres across. The mirror sculpture through which they had arrived stood in the middle of the circle, which was otherwise empty, and above the wall top was a serene and perfectly ordinary blue sky, with small white clouds drifting lazily across it.

There was only one way out of the circle, and that was through an arch set into the wall directly in front of them. The arch had double doors, firmly shut, and as if the violent pink wasn't bad enough, the doors were painted a hideously clashing lime green. Above the arch was a curving and very new-looking sign that read (in livid orange this time):

WELCOME TO THE QUEEN'S REALM

Winter said, 'What in the stars is *this* all about?'

Angel shook her head, lost for an answer, and they stepped towards the wall. Twinkle followed, but reluctantly, pressing close to Angel's ankles and making noises that sounded like a combination of muttering and growling. Reaching the wall, they touched it tentatively.

The wall wasn't made of stone, as they had first assumed.

It felt more like the thru-plast that Angel had grown up with, faintly spongy and pleasantly warm. She ran her hand over it, intrigued, and Winter gazed up at the sign. 'What do those letters say?' he asked.

Winter's efforts at reading were about as good as Angel's efforts at riding Pye's Personabiwheel; a contraption of handlebars and pedals and wheels that wouldn't even stand upright on its own. 'It's all right,' she told him. 'It doesn't spell out, "Prepare to Meet Thy Doom," or anything. Apparently, we're in The Queen's Realm.'

'The *Queen*? What sort of queen?'

She shrugged helplessly. 'I don't know. It doesn't say.'

'I don't call a hideous pink wall much of a realm,' Winter said. He eyed the double doors speculatively. 'That's the only way out, so we'd better see if we can get them open.'

'How?' Angel wanted to know. 'They look as if they're sealed, and there's no handle or ring; nothing at all.'

'Mmm . . .' Winter frowned. 'Well, we can only try, can't we?' Reaching out, he pushed a hand hard against one door, expecting to meet solid resistance. Instead, to his amazement, the entire door structure gave, then came loose from the arch and fell outwards with a dull slap.

Winter stared at the doors, which now lay forlornly at his feet. They were no more than a centi thick; he bent to touch them, and his voice was incredulous.

'They're *cardboard*!' This was crazy; it didn't make any sense; it—

Angel said, 'Winter . . .'

Quickly Winter looked up – and what he saw made him forget all about the doors.

The world beyond the pink wall was one of the most bizarre sights he had ever seen. Basically, it was a perfectly ordinary country landscape, with green grass, gentle rolling hills, trees and an utterly normal sun shining in an utterly normal sky. There were buildings, and paved paths, and a broad metal road running away into the distance to right and left. But the buildings were only about half the size they should have been, and each one was crazily different to all the others. There were cottages, castles, towers, pyramids; over to one side was a bridge that appeared to lead to and from nowhere, and in the farther distance a gigantic and rickety-looking wheel had been set up on end. Everything was painted in garish colours, flags flew from poles on the tops of most of the structures, and the wheel had been draped with ribbons that fluttered in the breeze.

And wherever they looked, there were notices. Scores of them, large and small, some mounted on wooden frames, others fixed to coloured poles and carved in the shape of pointing fingers.

'What . . .' Winter's voice came out as a squeak; he swallowed and tried again. 'What does that nearest notice say?'

Angel narrowed her eyes. ' "This way to . . ." ' Then she shook her head. 'The rest's too faded. I can't read it.'

'Oh.' He paused. 'Now you mention it, *everything*'s faded, isn't it? Look at that tower – half the colour's flaked off it. And the castle—'

'Castle?'

'Well, sort of; over there.' He pointed. 'Either it's only

half-finished, or half of it's fallen down. The whole place looks . . . abandoned.'

He was right, Angel realised. She hadn't fully taken it in before, but an uneasy feeling had been nagging at the back of her mind, and suddenly it clicked into focus. There was no one else here. No sign of movement, no trace of sound. People, animals, birds . . . there was nothing at all.

'Perhaps it's . . . closed, or something,' she suggested uneasily. 'Like the Playdomes in my world; they shut them sometimes, to do maintenance . . .'

Winter snorted. 'This place hasn't had any maintenance done to it for years! No; I think it *has* been abandoned.'

'So why is there a mirror doorway here? And that sign – "Welcome to the Queen's Realm". It wasn't faded like everything else; in fact it looked double-A new.' Angel rubbed at her arms, which had suddenly broken out into chillbumps. 'The people who were kidnapped must have come through that doorway. Where have they been taken? Where *are* they?'

'Maybe the kidnapper chose this place because it *is* abandoned,' Winter suggested. 'It makes logical sense, if he doesn't want anyone else to know what he's doing. I think we ought to look around and see if we can find any clues. And maybe we should start by trying to decipher some of those notices.'

She nodded, and tugged on the gold lead, pulling Twinkle away from her sniffing exploration of the grass. Twinkle said crossly, 'Don't want to! Pooey!' but Angel ignored the protest. They headed towards the nearest of the finger signs, a cluster of six fixed to the top of a tall pole and all pointing in different directions. Like everything else they were neglected and their paint faded, but most of the words on them were still legible.

' "Dare To Walk In The Haunted Wood",' Angel read aloud.

'Uh?' Winter was baffled.

'Don't ask! It sounds totally short-circuited to me, too.' She squinted at the next signs. ' "See The Magic Castle" . . . "To The Treetop Highway" . . . "Visit Santa's Grotto" . . .'

'Santa?' Winter cut in eagerly. 'Who's Santa? Could it be the kidnapper?'

Angel shrugged, then felt a quick surge of excitement. If they had a name to work on, then maybe—

She stopped, as she read the fifth notice. It said: 'This Way For Your FREE Ride To The Queen's Court'. The words were in a different style to all the others. They had obviously been painted very recently.

'Winter!' She grabbed his arm, the excitement bubbling over. 'This is it, this is the clue!' She recited the words to him, and his eyes lit.

'Come on, then! Let's do what it says, and take the ride!'

They started to run in the direction that the sign indicated. As the pink circular wall fell behind them Angel looked back once, wondering if it might be a dangerous mistake to venture too far away from the mirror doorway. It might be wiser to go back, report to Pye and get further instructions, in case—

'Angel, come *on!*' Winter was some way ahead. Angel

dithered, but only for a few moments before she turned and raced after him.

This notice was nailed to a rusting and tottery metal arch, and it read, in vivid purple letters:

FREE! FREE! FREE!
RIDES TO THE QUEEN'S COURT
ARE ALLOWED!
AND THEY'RE ABSOLUTELY FREE!!!

'This,' Winter said, 'just gets weirder and weirder . . .'

They were standing on a rectangle of ground with a hard, grey surface that reminded Angel of the pavewalks of Zone Bohemia. About four metres above their heads was a network of girders and cables that tangled and zig-zagged and criss-crossed each other like a demented spider's web. The girders all converged at the far side of the arena, and there they abruptly straightened and stretched away to vanish in the distance. It looked a little like the String monorail system, only a great deal less safe.

The Free Ride vehicles dangled from the girders. There were about twenty of them; little bubble-cars in a mad assortment of garish colours. They were held by cables, and a lot of the cables were frayed so that the cars swung alarmingly in the breeze.

'Well,' Winter said, 'If we want to get to this Queen's Court . . .'

'Frog that!' Angel retorted with feeling. 'I wouldn't trust any of those a single centi!'

'We'll have to, if we're not going to just give up and go home.' Winter walked under the girder network, peering up at one car after another. 'There must be some that are still safe . . . Ah! This one doesn't look too bad.'

She followed dubiously to where he stood beneath a blue-coloured car. It isn't easy to find a truly ugly shade of blue, but someone had managed it, and then compounded it by adding splodges of raspberry pink and fainting lilac all over the place. But at least it wasn't swinging around like the others.

'Come on,' said Winter. 'There's a ladder fixed to the upright over there.'

Angel stared at the car, stared at the ladder, then stared at him. She opened her mouth—

'Yowee!' said Twinkle excitedly. 'Go for a ride! *Fun!*' She tugged eagerly at her lead.

Angel was outnumbered. Sighing, and perfectly convinced that none of them was going to come out of this in one piece, she followed Winter towards the ladder.

The ladder was as rickety as it looked, but they climbed it without any disasters and made their way cautiously along the girder to the car. The car's top was open; Winter scrambled in, and – with misgivings – Angel followed. There was just enough room for two, though Twinkle's presence made it a bit of a squash. Angel gathered the Therapet on to her lap, and Twinkle goggled with enormous interest at the array of dials and switches on a panel beneath the front screen.

Winter was already fumbling under the panel. 'Right,' he said briskly. 'Now; if I'm not mistaken, there should be a startup control somewhere around here . . .'

He pressed something. A heartrending groan came from somewhere in the car's innards, followed by a loud creak. Then a row of lights sprang to life on the panel. Red, green and amber chased each other in a zig-zag pattern, and a voice announced, '*Welcome to the Queen's Realm! Are you ready for your free ride to the Queen's Court?*'

'It's got a computer!' Angel exclaimed. She couldn't begin to describe the relief she felt; here at last was something familiar, a technology she understood. It made this world seem a great deal safer.

'*Are you ready?*' the voice repeated, with possibly a tinge of impatience. '*You are allowed to answer.*'

'Yes, yes!' Winter told it. 'Ready.'

'*Thank you! Your startoff point is Line Seven, Slot Eighteen, and your car is called Bluebell! Hold on tight, now!*'

There was a judder, a lurch, and luckily Angel had the foresight to grab on to a convenient side rail an instant before the car leaped forward.

Winter yelped and grabbed for the opposite rail as the momentum slammed them both back in their seats. Twinkle squawked in alarm, and with her free hand Angel hung grimly on to the little cat as the car called Bluebell shot off along the monorail. In two secs they were clear of the arena; another two and they were rocketing through a chicane of other rails and girders at the edge of the entire tangle. Then they swung out at an insane angle, doubled back round a suicidal S-bend, straightened, and hurtled away down the straight track towards Tokyo alone knew what. Angel's shriek of terror was whipped away by the wind.

Back at the arena, the other cars gradually stopped shaking and juddering as everything settled down again. On one side of the arch where the welcome notice was nailed, a small box, which neither Angel nor Winter had noticed, clicked. And a shutter, which had been open on something resembling a round glass eye, slowly closed.

# SIX

Bluebell did slow down eventually, though 'slow' was still hardly the word for the pace at which they rushed and rattled along the monorail. Angel honestly thought that her teeth were going to be shaken loose by the bouncing and joggling: for all Winter's assurances, this felt about as safe as climbing up a twenty-metre metal pole in a thunderstorm. But as time went by and they didn't spectacularly crash, she began to relax a little and take in the landscape as it whizzed past.

There was no doubt that this reality had once been civilised. There were proper roads and buildings in the distance, and she could glimpse the metallic glints of other monorails here and there. But everything was overgrown, choked by grass and weeds and bushes . . . and there was still not a sign of life. No vehicles on the roads, no cars on the monorails; nothing whatsoever. It gave her the crawls.

Time passed, and still they sped on. Twinkle went to sleep (it was all right for her; she was snuggled down out of the airstream and wasn't getting blown to shreds) and Angel and Winter had nothing more to do than sit tight, hold on, and wait.

The chronometer on the gadget Pye had given to Winter told them that just over an hour had passed when the car began to joggle more violently and they realised

54

that they were slowing down again. A buzzing whine started up behind the panel and the computer started to say, '*We are now approaching*—' before something went wrong and the announcement collapsed into an electronic burp.

'There's a curve coming up,' Winter shouted over the whine and the wind noise. 'Hang on!'

Angel did, and felt as if her stomach was going one way while the rest of her went another as the car swerved round a loop. There was a change in the scenery ahead, but the sun was in her eyes and she couldn't see clearly what it was. The ground looked *blue* . . .

Then the car changed direction again, and she saw that the land wasn't land at all, because it was *moving*—

She grabbed Winter's arm so hard that he nearly fell out of the car in surprise. 'What's happened to the ground?' she yelled. 'Something's gone wrong!'

'It hasn't!' Winter shouted back. 'That's the sea – we've come to the coast!'

Angel's eyes widened. She had seen the sea in vids and Vee programmes, of course, but she had never actually visited it. In her reality people didn't go anywhere *near* real Nature, unless they absolutely had to; Nature was too dirty, too uncontrolled and too *dangerous*.

She stared, fascinated, as the car took them closer and closer, until the vista of a wide bay opened out before her. It was just like the tour-vids: a vast and glorious expanse of sapphire blue, glittering with sunlight and stretching away to the distant horizon. The bay formed a half-circle at its edge, and in the middle of the bay was an island. It looked absolutely idyllic . . . and there wasn't a living soul to be seen.

The car had slowed right down now, and was approaching a monorail terminus like a small version of the network at the start of their journey. It entered the tangle, zig-zagged into the middle of it, and stopped with sound so like a sigh of relief that Angel was quite touched. The computer said: '*Welcome to . . .*' but then gave up again. And suddenly the only sound was the surge and murmur of the sea.

For a minute or so they didn't move, but looked around them at the terminus. Like the one they had left, it was run down and neglected. Rust had eaten away a lot of the metal struts, and clusters of frayed cables, connected to nothing, dangled here and there like forlorn streamers after a carnival. Various notice-boards were dotted around, but even from a distance Angel could see that the lettering on them was too faded and eaten away for anything to be legible.

Except for one.

It was fixed to a tall pole at the top of which a piece of tattered fabric flopped, and it looked new. She could make out the word 'WELCOME' above some smaller and indistinct lettering, and there was a large scarlet arrow pointing towards the sea. Or, possibly, towards the island.

She drew Winter's attention to it, and he nodded. 'Looks like that's the way to go. Let's get out and have a closer look.'

Getting down from the car was easier than getting into it, as it had stopped, conveniently, right next to a ladder.

The ladder creaked and wobbled, and an alarming shower of rust flakes fell from the rungs as their feet touched them, but they made it safely to the ground. Twinkle shook herself and said, 'Pooey!', and Angel and Winter took deep breaths.

'What's that smell?' Angel asked, wrinkling her nose with distaste.

Winter smiled drily. 'The sea.'

'Does it always stink like that?'

'It's stronger because the tide's out and a lot of seaweed's uncovered. Anyway, it isn't a stink. It smells wonderful.'

Angel gave him a sceptical look. 'I suppose I'll get used to it.'

They walked towards the pole where the notice was pinned. Next to it, the remains of a wall formed a rampart between land and shore. There were buildings in the distance, once brightly-coloured but now faded to a uniform off-white, and a few metres away the wall was breached by a broad ramp that led down to the beach. Angel looked wonderingly at the mixture of sand and pebbles, then focused her gaze on the island. It was probably a couple of hundred metres beyond the tideline, and there appeared to be some sort of causeway leading to it. The arrow on the notice did indeed point to the island, and the wording was now clear.

THIS WAY TO THE QUEEN'S COURT!
Fun, Fun, Fun at the Queen's Castle!
Low Tide: You are Allowed to Cross by the Causeway
(No Charge)

High Tide: You are Not Allowed on the Causeway.
Take a Miniflit or Ask the Boatman (Small Fee)
THE QUEEN WELCOMES RESPECTFUL
TOURISTS.

'Boatman?' Winter said when Angel read the notice to him. 'I can't see any sign of a boat.'

'Well, it's low tide, isn't it? You just said so.' Angel wasn't sure that she'd have recognised a boat if she saw one. She wondered, too, what a Miniflit was, and guessed that it must have something to do with the single overhead monorail that ran from the terminus, out over the water, and lost itself somewhere among a clump of trees on the island. There were no supports along the way and the rail sagged horribly in the middle, making her think that, on the whole, a boat would definitely be preferable.

As for the comment about 'respectful' tourists . . . that was odd in the notice's otherwise cheery and welcoming tone. Angel was going to ask Winter what he thought of it, but he had already crossed to the ramp and was walking down to the beach. Angel hesitated, giving the notice one last, suspicious look, then followed him.

Sand was strange stuff to walk on, and she wasn't sure if she liked it. Twinkle certainly didn't, and made such a fuss that Angel had to pick her up and carry her. From the safe vantage of Angel's shoulder Twinkle glared and muttered at the sand, ears flat to her head. Then as they neared the tideline she looked at the sea and perked up.

'Blue,' she said. 'Pretty!'

'It's water,' Angel told her.

'Isn't! Too big.'

'Oh, it's water all right. Do you want to put your paws in and see?'

Twinkle *hated* getting wet, and she blinked uncertainly. 'Is it *really* water?'

'Sure is,' Winter, who had heard, called back.

'Pooey, then! Nasty; *I'm* not going near it!' She glowered at the horizon. '*Too* big.'

The little cat's idiocy released some of the tension that had been building up in Angel, and she smiled as she followed Winter to the start of the causeway.

It was tricky going. The causeway was built from large slabs of stone, and it had probably once been fairly smooth and even. Now though, many of the slabs were cracked or broken, and big tides had shifted and tumbled them, so that in places it was necessary to scramble to reach the next section. Angel puffed and panted, ignoring Twinkle's complaints, and tried not to look too often at the sea lapping just a metre or so away. She didn't know what to make of the sea. It *moved* so much, and the incoming waves unnerved her, though Winter said that they were very small compared with some he had seen. *People used to swim in this*, she thought. The idea didn't appeal to her in the least.

By the time they were halfway across, the island was looming large. It was, in fact, a single pinnacle of rock, rearing against the sky and topped by a cluster of oddly regular geometric shapes. As they drew nearer, Angel realised why. There was a building on top of the island. It looked as if it had grown out of the rock, and it vaguely resembled a castle; the geometric shapes were its towers and turrets. A path wound up the island's steep side towards it, and Angel's heart sank. It would be an absolute *spider* of a climb to reach the top! Surely this couldn't be the place they were looking for?

But it was. The causeway ended in a flight of stone steps that led up to a tiny, deserted harbour, and when they stepped up on to the harbour wall, her hopes about the castle were squashed as they came face to face with yet another notice.

## WELCOME TO THE QUEEN'S COURT!

This Way to the Castle
You are Not Allowed to use the Elevator because it is Out of Order.
You are Allowed to use the Path.
We Apologise for Any Inconvenience

'Oh, flackers!' Angel groaned. 'I don't *believe* this!'

Winter sighed. 'We haven't got any choice, have we? Anyway,' nodding to their right, 'if that's the elevator, I wouldn't fancy trying it.'

She looked. Half-hidden in a clump of ornamental shrubs was a large, rusty metal cabin. It sat, at a drunken angle, at the foot of a sloping rail that ran up the side of the island; the rail was ridged, and an enormous cogwheel was slotted wonkily into it, with a handle jutting from its hub.

Angel said, 'Ah . . .' She looked up at the castle, then at

the path. 'Oh, well. The sooner we start, the sooner it'll be over.'

She set Twinkle down, seeing no reason why the Therapet should be carried now that they were clear of the sea. Twinkle promptly disappeared into a clump of bushes; munching noises followed and hastily Angel hauled on the lead, pulling her back.

'No!' she said. 'Naughty! It might be poisonous.'

'Isn't,' Twinkle mumbled, her mouth full. 'Blackberries. Yum!'

'Well, you can't have any more now! Come on; we've got another walk to do.'

'Up there?' Twinkle asked, eyeing the castle.

'Yes, up there.'

'Long way.' But then she brightened. 'Maybe there'll be food!'

'Yes, yes, maybe there will. Come *on!*'

They set off up the path. As they left the harbour behind, a small box half-hidden in a clump of tall flowering plants swivelled slowly around, clicked in a satisfied sort of way, and closed its round shutter . . .

By the time they had climbed fifty metres from the harbour, they realised that the path had more than a few peculiarities of its own.

First, there were the singing stones. They were the pink ones, set at intervals into the path, and when they were trodden on, a host of tinny little voices began trilling a tune, accompanied by jingling bells. Angel and Winter both jumped violently the first time it happened, but by the third burst of song Winter had worked out the source.

'The pressure must trigger off some sort of mechanism,' he said. 'Look, there's another one: stand on it, and see what happens.'

Angel didn't answer. She was too busy staring at something that reared up out of the overgrown bushes ahead of them and to their left. It was – or was supposed to be – a human figure, with a brightly coloured face-make and a huge, grinning mouth. It seemed to be made of some plaster-like stuff, and here and there the plaster had crumbled away, revealing a wire frame underneath. As they approached, a creaking sound came from somewhere beneath the figure, and its arms jerked up in what was, presumably, supposed to be a cheery wave.

'HO, HO, HO!' came a cracked voice. 'I'M A CLOWN, AS YOU CAN SEE. DANCE AND SING AND LAUGH WITH ME! IF YOU LAUGH, THEN—' The voice expired in a groan, and the waving arms juddered to a stop. Then the figure tilted sideways with an appalling mechanical noise, and stuck at a forty-five degree angle.

Angel and Winter looked at each other, but neither of them could think of a single word to say. Angel threw a baffled and faintly pitying glance at the tipsy clown, and they trudged on upwards.

They were careful, now, to avoid the pink stones, but when they came to a place where a single slab lay right across the path, they couldn't help but tread on it. It looked harmless enough, but all the same Winter was cautious as he put a foot down . . .

A metal rod jerked in the bushes beside them, and a

two-dimensional wooden shape sprang up out of the greenery. It looked like a cross between a rabbit and a dragon, and its hinged mouth clacked while the two little wheels that were its eyes rolled in opposite directions. Angel yelped and jumped back, and Twinkle fluffed out her arti-fur tail and hissed furiously.

Winter took his foot off the stone and the wooden shape flopped back into the bushes with a dull thud. 'I think,' Winter said, 'that I'm getting the measure of this place . . .'

'Well, fifty creds to you!' Angel retorted. 'As far as I'm concerned, it's just mad!'

'It isn't. All of this—' he extended an arm in a sweeping gesture, 'is like one of those Playdomes in your world; you know, the parks where people go to have Leisure Experiences with different themes. The technology's cruder here, but the idea's pretty much the same.'

'You mean, this Queen's Realm is a Leisure Experience?'

'Yes. Or at least it was, until it was abandoned. Now, most of it's fallen apart, but a few things are still working.'

'Like the monorail cars.' Then Angel frowned. 'They've got onboard computers, but nothing else seems to have.'

'Maybe there isn't any power to run bigger computers,' Winter suggested. 'That thing that jumped up at us was mechanical, and so was the clown. And the singing stones could be, too. Mechanical things don't need an energy source to run them.'

'But the monorail needs power,' she objected. '*That* isn't mechanical; so where's the energy coming from?'

'I don't know. But I wouldn't mind guessing—' Winter broke off and started visibly as a loud, expiring wail came from somewhere off to their right.

'What in the stars was *that*?' He peered in the direction of the noise, craning to see over the tangled greenery.

'Whatever it is, it isn't happy.' Angel's gaze travelled upwards to the castle looming above them, then suddenly she grabbed his arm. 'Winter! Up there . . .'

A balustraded walkway surrounded the base of the castle – and on the walkway a dozen or so shapes had appeared. For the first few secs Angel thought they, too, were mechanical models. Then she realised how wrong she was.

'Oh, spiders . . .' She swallowed, hard. 'They're *real* . . .'

The line of living, breathing people stared down at them. Each one wore a gleaming helmet with a feathered plume bobbing at the crown, and each one was holding something that Angel recognised from history-vids.

She said in a small, quavering voice, 'They've got guns. They're *soldiers* . . .'

As if her words were a cue the soldiers raised their guns, and Angel and Winter found themselves looking straight down the barrels of twelve levelled weapons. It didn't matter that the soldiers were at least thirty metres away. Angel *knew* what guns could do, and she felt as if every muscle in her body was collapsing into a useless mush.

Winter, who had never even heard of a gun, started to say, 'What's the matter? Why all the—' but she hissed, '*Shut your programme!*' and elbowed his ribs so hard that it took the rest of his breath away.

Above them one soldier cleared his throat, then shouted in their direction.

'Halt! Who goes there?'

Angel didn't know whether or not to answer. If she did, she might say the wrong thing. If she didn't, it might be taken as suspicious. Either way, she thought wildly, she could blunder straight into disaster.

She was opening and shutting her mouth like a stranded fish but getting absolutely nowhere when the soldier shouted again.

''Scuse me! I said: "Halt, who goes there?" '

The next man in the line leaned towards him and hurriedly whispered something, and the first soldier looked chagrined. 'Oh,' he said, and raised his voice to Angel again. 'Sorry! I should have added: "Friend or foe?" '

Angel blinked rapidly. 'What?'

'*Friend or foe*,' the soldier repeated, enunciating slowly and carefully. 'Now you answer. It's the way proper Queens welcome their visitors, you see. All part of the fun!'

Angel was totally boggled by that, but Winter, who hadn't been aware of the danger in the first place, called out, 'We're friends!'

'Ah!' The soldier seemed relieved. 'That's all right, then! You're allowed to come in.' He turned smartly to face his companions. 'Friends approaching! Guard detaaaail . . . Ten *Shun!*' They all sprang smartly into line. 'Queen's Salute to friends! PRE-sent *arms!*' The guns swung up until they were pointing skywards. 'Ready saluuuute . . . *FIRE!*'

The guns did absolutely nothing. Instead, to Angel's utter astonishment, every man bawled 'BANG!!' at the top of his voice. The guns were shouldered, the soldiers made a salute of sorts – and then they all ran away around the side of the castle. The leader looked back just before he disappeared. He waved, called, 'Enjoy your visit!' and secs later every soldier was gone.

Angel stared at the place where the leader had been standing, while all her expectations turned upside-down and her brain tried to make sense of the resulting muddle.

'They're not soldiers at all,' she said at last. 'They're actors . . .'

'Actors?'

'You know; like celebs in a fict-movie. They said their lines, and when they'd said them they went away. They're just like the clown, and the wooden rabbit-thing.'

'Well, at least they're human,' said Winter. 'So we know we're not the only living souls in this world.' He took hold of her hand. 'Come on. It's obvious that no one here means us any harm, so let's go on up to the castle and see who else we can find.'

Angel wanted to counsel caution, for a deep-rooted intuition was telling her that things were not quite as straightforward, or as harmless, as they appeared. But she couldn't put the feeling into words; it was too vague, and there was no obvious logic to back it up. So she said nothing as Winter led her onwards.

Another hundred metres brought them to the castle's main gate. There had been no more surprise encounters, human or otherwise, and the gate stood widely and welcomingly open. Beyond it they could see an empty courtyard, with a large, arched doorway, also wide open, at the far side.

Angel looked queryingly at Winter, who shrugged. 'No venture, no gain, as Pye would say. Ready?'

'I suppose so.' Angel wound Twinkle's lead a turn or two around her hand to be on the safe side, and they stepped through the gateway.

Nothing moved and no voices challenged them as they crossed the courtyard, and it did not take them long to realise that the castle wasn't the grandiose fortress that it had seemed from a distance. In fact, the whole structure was as tacky and artificial as everything else they had seen in this bizarre play-world. Most of the walls were made of plastic, and the rest appeared to have been patched together from a motley assortment of materials: wood, wire, plaster, cloth – you name it, someone had used it. Inside the building itself, things were crazier still. The place appeared to be a maze of passages, tunnels and staircases, all leading off at unlikely angles. Some walls had partly collapsed and leaned at drunken angles, one flight of stairs was only half-finished and ended in mid-air, and there was a large hole in the ceiling, with a pile of rubble beneath that suggested a recent cave-in.

They crossed a slightly sticky plastic floor that sagged alarmingly under their feet, and reached the largest of the tunnels. A notice hung there: in luminous letters it said, 'THIS WAY TO THE THRONE CHAMBER.'

It was a clue of sorts, so they followed the direction of the pointing arrow beneath the lettering. There followed a series of twists and turns as further notices led them on.

Within a couple of mins Angel had lost all sense of direction; for all she knew, they could go round and round in circles until they dropped from exhaustion. Twinkle was complaining that she was hungry, and Angel was just about to say to Winter that they were getting nowhere, when ahead of them a petulant voice said, 'Hurry up!'

They stopped, and Angel tugged on Twinkle's lead to silence her. The Therapet looked indignant, but she stopped grumbling and they all listened.

'I said, hurry *up!* I haven't got all day!'

The voice was some way off and muffled by the intervening walls, but there was no mistaking its humanity. Someone *was* here, and before Angel could stop him, Winter shouted back.

'Hello! Where are you?'

There followed what could best be described as a shrieking silence. It lasted for perhaps five secs – then they distinctly heard the sound of footsteps scurrying away.

'Winter, you flea!' Angel hissed. 'You've scared them off! How could you be so *dumb?*'

'I didn't know, did I?' Winter protested. 'At least we've found out that that there's someone around, and they're not far away.' He set off again and she rolled her eyes heavenwards in exasperation before stamping after him.

One final notice and one final turn in the corridor – and abruptly they came face to face with the Throne Chamber. They knew it was the Throne Chamber, despite the fact that the doors were shut, because a large plaque had been fixed above the lintel, proclaiming the name in erratically flashing pink neon.

'They've got working energy!' Angel exclaimed.

Winter nodded. 'There's probably a generator in the building; just enough to run a few circuits.' He had learned about generators from Pye. 'Mind you, it's obviously not working too well, or . . .'

He stopped. From the far side of the Throne Chamber door, a voice was calling.

'Coo-ee! Hel-lo-oh?' The tone was female, high-pitched and more than a little nervous.

And Angel's face turned pale.

'Hello?' the voice called again. '*Ohhh* . . . I *know* you're there, so *please* answer, or you'll make things even more difficult! Look, sweeties, I'm sorry, but I can *never* remember what I'm supposed to say, so just give me a *teeny* prompt, yes?'

Angel said in a quavering wail, 'Winter . . .'

He didn't understand; didn't realise the significance of what they were hearing. His hand reached for the door. It was cardboard, and he could easily have put a fist straight through it, but it seemed more polite not to make a drama of their entrance. As the door wobbled back on its frayed hinges, the unseen occupant of the Throne Chamber burst out angrily:

'Oh, *flackers!* This is turning into a *major* trauma, and if someone doesn't do something, I shall have an absolute *Episode!*'

The door was half-open, and suddenly Angel pushed past Winter and ran in.

The Throne Chamber was enormous, and decorated with a vast array of banners and flags. They hung on the walls, they dangled from the ceiling, they were draped over the rail and banisters of the wide, pillared staircase that curved up to a broad gallery high above. Angel didn't see them. She could only stare fixedly at the Throne itself – a colossal chair covered with excrutiating gold and silver glitter and crude fake jewels, that was set on an equally bad-taste plinth in the middle of the floor. Someone was sitting in the chair. She wore a dazzlingly hideous gown of shimmering fabric in six garish colours, and in one hand was a spangled wand which she haplessly waved around as if it ought to do something. Her black-and-green striped hair was piled up on her head, and set precariously on top of the pile was a silver-coloured crown with points nearly a metre high.

She stared at Angel. Angel stared at her.

'*Mother . . . ?*' Angel squeaked.

## SEVEN

Soho's eyes widened until they looked as if they would pop right out of her skull. '*Who?*' she said. 'Oh *really*! You're not the least bit like my daughter, you absolutely are *not*. This is *ridiculous*!'

'Mother!' Choking on the cry, Angel dropped Twinkle's lead and ran to the Throne. She held out her arms, but Soho made an exasperated noise and batted at her with the wand.

'No, no, NO!' she exploded. 'I absolutely and totally and utterly *refuse* to play a scene about Angel! Nobody told me we were going to do it, and I haven't had *any* chance to rehearse!'

'Scene?' Angel wailed. 'Rehearse? Mother, this isn't a fict! It's real, it's *me*! I'm Angel, I'm your *daughter*!'

'Of course you're not!' Soho snorted. 'Look at you – that make, that hair, those *appalling* clothes! You're just a pretend Angel, and a very bad one at that. Ohh, this is *too* much!' She waved the wand again, energetically. 'You're a new one, aren't you? You must be; and they've told *you* to play my daughter but they didn't bother to tell *me*, let alone show me the script! How can anyone *possibly* expect me to be Queen when I haven't even seen the *script*?'

Angel's jaw dropped. 'You're – you're the Queen?'

'Yes, yes, yes! Or at least I'm *supposed* to be; it's my role,

71

you see, but everything's so disorganised that I don't think my nerves can stand it for much longer! I need an *understudy*, but—'

'Hover a min!' Winter had caught up with Angel and was now standing beside her. 'What do you mean, it's your role? Are you the Queen, or aren't you?'

'No,' said a sharp, light voice from the gallery above them. 'She's only a pretend Queen. *I'm* the real one.'

A small figure appeared at the top of the sweeping staircase. She was dressed entirely in silver, and her hair was so blonde that it seemed to blend with the high, fan-like collar of her dress. Her face was kittenish, the skin pale and flecked with freckles. She couldn't have been more than ten years old.

'I am Queen Tertia,' she said, glowering at them both with eyes like hard little emeralds. 'And you'd better tell me right *now* how you got into my world without being invited!'

Winter was so astonished that he simply stood gawping at the silver vision. Angel, though, had more self-possession – and she didn't take kindly to being spoken to in that tone by a child.

'Without being invited?' she echoed indignantly. 'I wasn't aware we needed your *personal* permission. What about all the "welcome" signs?'

Tertia turned from Winter to rake her with a searing look. 'What's your name?' she demanded.

Angel glared back. 'Angel.'

'Your Majesty.'

'What?'

' "Angel, Your Majesty". I'm the queen, so that's what you have to say whenever you speak to me.' She folded her arms, and her voice grew icy. 'Go on; say it. Or I just might get *cross*.'

Angel's temper started to rise. But over Tertia's shoulder Winter noticed a look of horror and fear appear on Soho's face, and an intuitive alarm bell rang in his mind. He nudged Angel's side before she could say what she was about to, and hissed under his breath, '*Don't argue with her – say it!*'

Angel hesitated – then to Winter's relief she shrugged irritably. 'Oh, all right, if it makes her happy! Angel, Your *Majesty*.'

'That's better.' Tertia didn't seem to notice the sarcasm in Angel's voice. 'Don't forget again. Forgetting isn't allowed. So: I'd better decide what I'm going to do with you, hadn't I?' She started to walk in a circle around them, studying them both critically. 'You' – she jabbed a small finger at Winter – 'whatever you're called – might make quite a good courtier. But *you*,' she all but sneered at Angel, 'are more like—' Then abruptly her voice tailed off, and her eyes focused at floor level. 'What,' she said, 'is *that*?'

Twinkle had been so busy gawping at Tertia that, for once, she hadn't said a single word. Now though, as the girl's attention switched to her, she blinked and stated cheerfully, 'I'm Twinkle, and I'm hungry. Can I have some food?'

Tertia continued to stare for several more secs. Her face was unreadable; she might have been furious or just plain

73

baffled. Then suddenly and unexpectedly, her face broke into a smile.

'A talking cat!' she said. 'I like it! Yes; I'll have it in my court. Come here, cat.'

She snapped her fingers at Twinkle, and Angel's voice went up indignantly. 'Hover a min! For one thing Twinkle's a Her, not an It, and for another she's ours, so you can't just announce that you'll have her and spiders to everyone else!'

Tertia's hand stopped still and her eyes came up to meet Angel's, quite slowly but with a new look in them that made Angel's skin prickle. '*I*,' she said, 'can do whatever I like. You'd better remember that, because if you don't, I will *definitely* get cross.' She flicked a vicious glance in Soho's direction. '*She* knows what I mean. I've been cross with her twice, and she didn't like it one bit.'

Soho's face under its make had turned a sickly shade of grey-green; she nodded rapidly at Angel and her eyebrows made frantic pleading signals. The air felt electric suddenly, and the feeling was so strong that Angel had the ugly impression that some real energy had been released into the Throne Chamber, like a poisonous gas.

'Look,' she started, mentally backpedalling, 'I didn't exactly mean—'

'Shut up,' said Tertia. 'I'm not interested in *you*.' She looked down at Twinkle again and repeated, 'Come here, cat. You'd like some food, would you?'

'Yum!' Twinkle agreed eagerly.

'What sort of food do you like best?'

That stumped Twinkle; basically, she would eat anything

that didn't make her sick, and quite a few things that did. Her ears flattened out sideways and she thought hard for a sec or two before venturing, 'Ice cream . . . ?'

Tertia clapped her hands. 'Good! I shall have ice cream, too. We shall *all* have ice cream! You!' to Soho. 'We're playing the banquet game now. Tell the servants to fetch ice cream.'

'Oh,' said Soho. 'Yes, Your Majesty. Um . . . what flavour?'

'Roasted swan. Swans are very royal. Come on, come on; play! *Now!*'

'Um, yes, absolutely . . .' Soho fumbled behind the throne and produced a rather large handbell. It took some effort to lift, and when she rang it, it made a cracked, doleful sound that sent Angel's ears aching. As the noise died away, running footsteps sounded outside the room and moments later a man and a woman appeared. They both wore what was clearly supposed to be some kind of livery, cobbled together out of an assortment of fabrics with some paper thrown in for good measure. They looked unutterably ridiculous.

'We come at your bidding, O Queen!' they chorused breathlessly. The words, and the bows that went with them, were addressed to Soho, but they eyed Tertia nervously as they recited.

'Um,' said Soho. 'Yes. We're playing the banquet game. I – ah – want some ice cream. Um. Pickled . . . no, what was it?'

'Roasted!' Tertia snapped.

'Oh, yes, of course; silly me!' Soho gave a peculiar, high-pitched laugh. 'Roasted swan flavour.'

'And you want it *now*,' prompted Tertia.

'Oh yes, I do, don't I? Abso*lutely*. I want it *now*. Yes. Er . . . thank you.'

'You don't say thank you to servants!' Tertia barked. 'How many times do I have to tell you? It's not allowed!'

Soho, looking distinctly ill by this time, mumbled an apology, and the two liveried servants stared helplessly at each other.

'Roasted swan . . .' the woman repeated in a small voice. 'Yes, O Queen.'

They both made another bow, and fled.

A dire silence descended when they had gone. Tertia stood with her arms folded and a frown on her face, Soho sagged back on the ludicrous Throne and shut her eyes, and Angel and Winter were too bemused to do anything except stare at the nearest wall. Only Twinkle seemed unfazed. Angel had dropped her lead and she was happily exploring the floor, sniffing every centi with vast interest. Tertia meanwhile, began an infuriating slow countdown.

'. . . Ten,' she said. 'Eleven. Twelve.' She started to tap one foot, in a totally different rhythm to her counting. It set Angel's teeth on edge.

'Thirteen. Fourteen. Fifteen.'

*Stop it!* Angel thought.

'Sixteen. Seventeen.'

*For Tokyo's sake, will you stop DOING that!!*

Finally Tertia reached one hundred and forty-seven, and Angel's nerves were coming very close to snapping point, when running footsteps sounded again and the two servants returned.

Pye had introduced Angel and Winter to the delights of ice cream, and what the servants were carrying on a large tray between them bore no resemblance to it whatsoever. Angel looked at the heaped grey mess, which had green feathers sticking out of the top for decoration, and firmly shut off any speculation about what might have gone into it. Tertia, though, stopped tapping her foot, and beamed at everyone.

'Ice cream!' she said, and snapped her fingers towards the tray. 'Let the banquet begin!'

Angel stared at the mucky heap. 'That isn't ice cream!'

Tertia's small green eyes turned arctic. 'It's whatever I say it is!' she retorted. 'I'm Queen here. This is *my* game, and everyone plays by *my* rules, or I'll—'

'Get cross? Oh, double-A – I'm *really* impressed!'

Before the words came out, a small inner voice told Angel not to say them. But she couldn't stop herself. She was wound up like a spring at top tension: the combination of encountering Soho with this obnoxious child, in a place that was nothing short of completely insane, was simply too much for her self-control.

And losing her self-control was a big mistake.

Tertia stopped as if she had been switched off, with her mouth still forming the word 'cross'. She stared at Angel. Then her eyes changed their focus, and for a shockingly disorientating moment she seemed to look straight through Angel and out the other side. She didn't speak, but she did smile – the most chilling smile Angel had ever seen.

Then Tertia raised her right hand, and pointed.

It felt to Angel as though huge, invisible hands had reached down out of the sky and grabbed her under the arms. She was whisked into the air, and her yell of shock echoed round the Throne Chamber as she hung dangling and kicking with her feet two metres above the floor.

'*Noo!*' she screeched. '*Put me down!*'

'Shut up,' said Tertia. She made a negligent gesture with her left hand, and one of the tall and impressive staircase pillars started to rock wildly. There was a groan, a noise like paper ripping, and the pillar tore loose from its fixing and fell to the floor. It was only made of cardboard, but the effect as it bounced and rolled was spectacular nonetheless.

'See what you've done?' Tertia put her fists on her hips and looked up at Angel. 'You've made me *cross*.'

Angel wondered desperately if she was going to be sick. As Tertia was standing directly beneath her, she prayed it wouldn't happen.

Tertia made another gesture, and three of the garish banners slid off the walls, bringing a chunk or two of flimsy plaster with them. Then she turned to look at Soho. Soho had shrunk back on the Throne, her face fixed in an ingratiating smile that made her look like a corpse.

'It wasn't me,' she gushed. 'Really, Your Majesty, it wasn't me, I didn't invite them, I don't even know who they are, and . . . oh dear . . . er . . . isn't this game *fun*?'

'Shut up,' Tertia said again. Her hand flicked, and Soho's enormous silver crown started to spin. Soho squealed as the points caught and tangled in her hair; then Tertia made another gesture and the crown stopped spinning and jammed itself hard down over Soho's eyes.

'Right,' said Tertia. She looked up at Angel once more. 'You get the message do you?'

Angel made an inarticulate noise.

'Good. I'm bored with this game. Serve the ice cream!'

The two liveried servants were standing rigid, their faces expressionless, but at this command they jumped and started to ladle the contents of the tray out in heaps on the floor. Twinkle homed in and pushed her face into the first pile. Slurping noises followed, then the Therapet announced, 'Yum! Nice!'

Tertia smiled at her. '*Good* cat,' she said, then pointed to another heap and gave Winter a sly look. 'There's yours. Eat it.'

Winter nodded nervously. 'Yes . . . Your Majesty.' He sat down cross-legged on the floor. 'Have you . . . ah . . . got any spoons?'

'We use pretend spoons here, like the pretend tables and chairs. *Eat.*'

Angel, still dangling, watched numbly as Winter dipped a shaking finger into the gooey mess. She saw his face screw up as he tasted it, and he seemed to have difficulty swallowing.

'Not like *that*,' said Tertia scornfully. 'Haven't you ever been taught manners? Watch me!'

She dropped to a crouch before another pile of the stuff, and started to mime eating with an imaginary spoon. Her mouth opened and closed and she made appreciative noises, but she didn't actually touch any of the stuff.

'Ah . . .' said Winter. 'I *see* . . .'

'Go on, then. You're allowed.' Abruptly Tertia remembered Angel and looked up again. 'You're allowed, too.' She snapped her fingers, and with no warning whatever, the force that had been holding Angel vanished. She dropped like a stone, landing with a thump that made the floor sag and brought down two more banners. Tertia smirked unpleasantly at her.

'I'm not cross any more,' she said. 'That's lucky for you, isn't it?'

'Y-y-y-y . . .'

'Your Majesty.'

'Y-your M-m-m-m . . .'

But Tertia had lost interest. She strode to the Throne, snatched Soho's glittering wand and then walked away towards the staircase, waving the wand as if conducting some silent and invisible orchestra. Winter scrambled to where Angel was trying to sit up. 'Are you all right?' he hissed.

'Yes, I th-think so . . . Tokyo, what did she *do* just then?'

'I don't know. She produced a kind of energy field, or something.' Tertia was now standing in front of the fallen pillar, waving the wand at it and frowning when nothing happened, and Winter glanced cautiously towards Soho. 'Your mother . . .'

Soho had managed to unwedge the crown and was very obviously doing Anti-Trauma breathing exercises. Angel felt a wave of misery.

'She didn't even recognise me, Winter. She thinks we're both fict actors . . .'

Winter's eyes narrowed. 'That's not surprising, is it?

Because everyone here *is* a fict actor, Soho included. All the talk about games and scripts – the whole thing's just one great artificial scene, with that child directing it all.'

The connection clicked in Angel's mind. 'And the people who've been disappearing are all celebs . . .'

'Right. She's kidnapping ready-made stars for her crazy scenarios.'

'But how's she *done* it? The energy force, the *power* – where does it come from?'

'I couldn't even start to guess,' said Winter. 'Listen, I think we should try to get out of here and back to our own world. We can't tackle this on our own. We need Pye.'

Angel looked at Soho again. She didn't like the idea of leaving her, but Winter was right: Pye's help was vital if they were going to put a stop to Tertia's games. And games were all Tertia seemed to want. Provided Soho went along with them, played her role and did what she was told – which seemed likely – she would come to no harm.

'All right,' Angel said. 'So, the first thing to do is work out how to get off the island. Maybe if we—'

'*DAMN* you!'

The shout, accompanied by a hollow banging, cut her off, and they saw that Tertia had tired of trying to magic the pillar upright with the wand, and had resorted instead to kicking it viciously where it lay. There were already several holes in the cardboard, and Tertia's face was turning an alarming shade of red.

Then the tantrum vanished as suddenly as it had begun. Tertia gave the pillar one final jab with a silver-slippered foot, blew out a long breath, turned on her heel and came marching back to where Angel and Winter sat.

'Everyone has had enough ice cream,' she declared. 'No one's allowed any more.' She pointed at Twinkle, who was starting on her third pile of grey goo. 'Including her.'

Twinkle looked up with both cheeks bulging, and Angel grabbed the opportunity to haul her away from her feast. The cat tried to object, but Angel clamped her jaws firmly shut.

'Now,' said Tertia, clasping her hands together. 'What game shall we play next?' She turned and studied Soho critically. 'You're not being a very good pretend Queen today, so I think I'll find something else for you to do.'

Soho looked as if she couldn't decide whether to be relieved or worried. 'Um, yes . . .' she said. 'Could I – uh – ask what, exactly?'

'Oh, I'll think of something. Gardening, probably. So: I want a new pretend Queen, don't I? Or maybe . . .' She glanced over her shoulder, and this time her smile had a positively coquettish slant. 'Maybe a pretend Handsome Prince . . . ?'

This time, Angel was wise enough not to yell out a furious protest. Winter had learned his lesson, too, but as he realised what Tertia had in mind his face blanched and a look of sheer horror came into his eyes. Seeing the look, Tertia smiled.

'Oh, *yes*,' she said with enormous satisfaction. 'You'll do nicely, and *she*' – meaning Angel – 'doesn't like it, does she? That's fine, because I don't like *her*. Come on, come on,' to Winter. 'Try the Throne for size.' She raked Soho with a glare. 'You, get off. Curtsey to the Handsome Prince, then go and do some gardening, like I told you.'

Angel had never seen Soho move so fast. She positively jumped off the Throne and the platform, tripped over the hem of her skirt, righted herself and made a grovelling gesture in Winter's direction.

'Take that stupid crown off,' Tertia told her.

Soho flung the crown away. It landed with a dull thud on the floor, and two of the spikes broke off.

'Garden,' said Tertia meaningfully.

Soho fled. Angel saw her disappear through the door, heard her footsteps retreating, and thought: *I'm going to wake up in a a min. I've got to, because this can't possibly be real* . . .

'That's better.' Tertia walked in a circle around the Throne, where Winter was now sitting. 'Mmm,' she said at last. 'You need some proper Handsome Prince clothes, but apart from that I'm quite pleased with you. I suppose you're going to be just like the others, and have to be told what to do all the time.'

'I don't—' Winter began, but another glare silenced him.

'They all want these stupid scripts,' said Tertia. 'It's boring, but I suppose it's because they're famous, and famous people aren't very intelligent.' She stopped circling and her eyes narrowed. '*You're* famous, aren't you?'

Winter looked uncertainly at Angel, who replied quickly, 'Oh yes, he's famous. We both are.'

'I don't care about you,' said Tertia. 'I'm only interested in the Handsome Prince. In fact . . .' she paused, and to Angel's discomfort walked a few paces towards her. 'In fact, I've decided that *you're* not allowed to be famous.

83

You're just a Thing, and you can't have a part in the games. Go away.'

'What?'

'You heard me. Go away. Out of my Throne Chamber.'

If Angel had felt distinctly unreal before this moment, the feeling was redoubled now. In disbelief she watched Tertia turn away, dismissing her as though she simply didn't exist. Winter, on the Throne, was trying to mime and mouth some message at her, but Angel was too numb to take it in. This was totally, utterly and incredibly *mad*. She *would* wake up in a min. *Surely* she would?

But Angel knew this wasn't a dream. Tertia was walking around Winter again, muttering under her breath; Angel half-raised a hand as if to catch her attention, but Tertia ignored her and the hand flopped helplessly to her side again.

'Come on, cat,' Tertia said to Twinkle. 'You'll be the Handsome Prince's Magic Cat. Sit on his knee.'

Twinkle looked at Tertia, then at Angel, clearly confused. Angel wanted to run to her and snatch her up, but Winter gave a sharp, warning shake of his head. This time when he mimed something, Angel got it. It was just one word, but the message was clear. Winter was mouthing, '*Pye!*' Then he said aloud, 'Come on, Twinkle. I'll look after you. This game's going to be fun, isn't it?'

Angel understood. Winter was reassuring her that he had the sense to play along with Tertia, which meant that he and Twinkle would come to no harm. Angel stole one more glance at the child, who was humming a little tune now, slightly off key, obviously absorbed in her plans for the Handsome Prince and His Cat.

*Get out of here*, an inner voice told Angel. *Fast.*

She started to tiptoe towards the Throne Chamber door, then realised that Tertia was oblivious to her departure, and ran for it.

# EIGHT

How Angel found her way outside she never quite knew, but somehow, after tangling herself in a maze of passages, blind turnings and unused rooms, she emerged through an arched door (it was actually a rectangular door, but someone had tacked plastic curves on to make it look Olde) and into what was clearly the Queen's Garden.

Breathing hard, and aware of her heart pumping overtime, she stared around. She was faced with another maze of paths and shrubberies that fell away down the rocky slope of the island. Most of the paths either doubled back on themselves or looked as if they ended abruptly in a sheer drop, and Angel couldn't see a clear way down. She tried to pick out the track they had used on the climb from the harbour, but it was impossible; for all she could tell, it might be on the island's far side and completely inaccessible from here. But she had to find it. She had to get *out* of this place, back to the mirror doorway, back to Pye . . .

She threw a glance over her shoulder to the arched door, but decided that she dared not risk retracing her steps. She'd been lucky so far; she had heard distant sounds of people moving about, but nobody had suddenly appeared round a corner and told her that running away Wasn't Allowed. She didn't want to push that luck too far.

Safer to stay on the outside. But that meant tackling the dizzying slope ahead of her . . .

She was still dithering when, from a short distance away, a voice rose up in a wail of melodramatic anguish:

'Ohh . . . FLACKERS!'

Angel snapped her head round just in time to see Soho rising like one of the mechanical figures from a nearby bush.

Soho was still wearing her garish Pretend Queen's gown, but an enormous apron was now swathed over it, making her look vaguely like a balloon. In place of the crown, the outfit was topped by a vast mauve bonnet; her face under the bonnet was a picture of tragedy, and she was sucking at one finger.

'It isn't *fair!*' she lamented, her voice muffled by the finger. 'I haven't *rehearsed* gardening, and these things are so − so − well, whatever they are, they *hurt!*' Suddenly then she saw Angel, and tragedy gave way to petulance. 'You again! This is *all* your fault! If you absolute *juveniles* hadn't skimmed in and spoiled everything, I wouldn't be out here, being attacked by these *horrible* plant things! I'm going to have a Traumatic Episode, I *know* I am!'

'I'm sorry!' Angel scrambled through the shrubbery towards her. *Okay, you know you're not going to wake up now, but keep pretending it isn't real. It's the only way to say sane . . .* 'We didn't mean to spoil your . . . your role. We don't even want to *be* here; we just want to go home!'

Soho flapped a hand at her. 'Well, *go* home, then!'

'I don't know how! You've got to help me!'

'Help?' Soho looked surprised and a little offended.

87

'Well, I don't know about that, sweetie. If anyone owes anyone a favour, then I think *you* owe *me*, yes? After all, you utterly ruined—'

'I *know*, and I *said* I'm sorry!'

'Ohh!' Soho's long-suffering pose would have sent a vidfict producer into raptures. 'I keep telling you, I haven't *seen* this script before! But all right – if no one takes the trouble to tell me, who am I to argue? I suppose all true celebs have to suffer for their art, and—'

'*Just tell me how to get out of this place!*' Angel yelled.

Soho blinked. 'Through the Vee-door, of course! Oh, *really*, this game is *mega*-crass!'

Clinging to her self-control, Angel said through clenched teeth, 'This isn't Vee, so there isn't a Vee-door! I need to find the path down to the causeway, and then—'

'The causeway?' Soho interrupted. 'Sweetie, reorganise your circuits! Only a sec ago you said you wanted to go home, wherever *that* is, and now suddenly you're rewinding the entire vid and telling me you want to go to another part of this Vee!' She heaved a vast, long-suffering sigh. 'Tokyo, I hate working with amateurs! I swear, I shall fire my agent; he must be out of his *mind*—'

'This is *not* Vee!' Angel persisted.

But Soho wasn't listening; she had drawn up her shoulders and was breathing deeply and dramatically. After three or four breaths she relaxed. '*That's* better. Calm-calm-calm: *Power-breathe every day, And trauma floats away* . . . All right, we'll run again. You want to go home: that's the line, yes?'

'Yes!'

'Then it's perfectly simple, isn't it? Go out through the Vee-door in New Players' Reception. For Tokyo's sake, it's only centis away from where you're standing!'

'What . . . ?' said Angel, very softly.

'*The Vee-door!*' Soho repeated, as if she was talking to an idiot. 'Where we all came in when we got our contracts? Remember, sweetie?' She rolled her eyes skywards. 'Where did they *find* you? I can't believe you're a celeb; you're about as bright as a defective Therapet! Now, I really am *tired* of this. Just go through that door,' pointing back to the castle, 'turn left – you *do* know the difference between left and right, I presume? – to New Players' Reception, and *flit*.' She scowled. 'And if you're penalised for breaking your contract, it serves you right. *Amateurs*!'

She turned her back huffily on Angel, and marched away with as much dignity as her costume allowed.

*The Vee-door, where we all came in* . . . Angel's heart started to race again as a part of the puzzle clicked into place. Soho – and probably all the other abductees – believed that this whole world was a Virtual Reality scenario. Tertia must have played some pretty elaborate tricks on them, Angel thought. She had probably gate-crashed media parties, maybe even slipped a potion or two into the glitter-ice drinks, then conned her victims into believing that she was the child of some multinational mega-producer, and her Prime Parent was avid to sign them up for her latest vid-fantasy at a vast salary. But what mattered more – the only thing that mattered, in fact – was that Tertia had a second doorway between realities. And that second doorway was right here in the castle.

What had Soho said? 'Turn left to New Players' Reception'. Soho was out of sight now (though a large shrub was shaking and rustling a short way off, as if someone or something was tangled up in the middle of it). For a moment Angel hesitated, wondering if she could persuade her mother to go with her. But it was pointless. For all her traumas and complaints, Soho was probably having the time of her life; she wouldn't dream of agreeing.

Angel turned and ran back into the castle.

She found what she was looking for, if not exactly centis away at least close enough to make her wonder how in the stars she had managed to miss it on her way out. Calling herself a spidering fool, and a cross-eyed bat into the bargain, Angel pushed open the door with its large, badly written notice proclaiming: 'NEW PLAYERS RECEPTION. ADMITTANCE WITHOUT PERMISSION IS NOT ALLOWED', and went in.

There was only one object in the room, and she recognised it at once. A structure made of metal and mirrors, angled so that they reflected the light from a high window in a thousand fragmented reflections. There were no water jets, though, and Angel approached cautiously, wondering if this mirror doorway worked in exactly the same way as Pye's or if there was some subtle – and possibly dangerous – difference. Multi-images of her own face stared back at her as she examined the structure. Could she open the doorway? And, if she could, what sort of world would she find herself stepping into? The scanner Pye had given them was in her pocket, but she hadn't listened properly to his instructions and had no idea how to use it. She wished Winter was with her, but he wasn't, and she had to make her mind up either to take the jump, wherever it led, or find another way out of this reality. Which meant getting off the island, into one of the terrifying monorail cars (assuming she could make *that* work, which she probably couldn't) and all the way back to the abandoned Playdome from where they had started. Oh, *Flackers!*

She reached towards the mirror structure, hesitated, reached again, hesitated again. A long string of 'what ifs' lurked like menacing monsters in the back of her mind, and she couldn't make a decision—

Until it was made for her, as from somewhere in the castle's depths came an angry shout.

'*I'm the Queen, and we'll play whatever game I say we will! Do you want me to get cross?*'

Tertia . . . Angel jumped, then tensed, listening hard. She heard another voice, whining and fawning – not Winter or Soho, thankfully, but a stranger – then Tertia snapped, 'I don't *care* if the cat scratched you! It's *my* cat, and it wants *food*, and it's your role to *feed* it! Now, *move!*'

Two sets of footsteps. One set hurried away, fading as it went.

The other set sounded as if it was heading straight for this room.

Panic hit Angel, squashing the 'what ifs' out of existence. She swung to face the mirrors, reaching out to them again, so that her multi-reflections loomed suddenly larger and closer.

Light flared in New Players' Reception, and Angel

vanished as Tertia, unaware of what had just happened, swept past the door.

'Oh,' said a voice, with a distinct note of unease in it. 'You again . . .'

Angel blinked, and realised that she was standing knee-deep in water. Then her vision cleared and she saw where the doorway had brought her.

She was in the fountain, in the bizarre park, in the world where almost everyone told lies. In front of her, sitting on the back of her familiar half-painted horse, was Suuu Beeen Aaat.

Suuu's hair was purple today, matching the horse's newly-dyed colour. 'Damn,' she said. 'I saw that someone was coming through, but I didn't imagine it would be *you*. I suppose Pye sent you, after what happened last time.'

'Pye didn't send me,' replied Angel, splashing out of the fountain and squelching to where Suuu waited. The horse whickered and pushed an inquisitive, snuffing nose towards her, but she ignored it and stared Suuu challengingly in the face. 'I've been to Tertia's world. *Queen* Tertia, that is. And you know exactly who I mean.'

Suuu's expression changed rapidly, and she heartily wished that this wasn't one of her truth times. Thinking quickly, she decided that it was safest to say nothing – silence wasn't a lie, after all – and clamped her mouth firmly shut.

Angel, though, wasn't going to be put off. 'You *do* know who I mean,' she repeated. 'And I know now why you're so scared of her.'

'Ah,' Suuu looked down at her left foot and swung it restlessly in the stirrup. 'Right.' She glanced up. 'What did she do to you?'

'Enough.' Angel didn't want to tell anyone about the indignity Tertia had inflicted on her when she got *cross*. 'I got away, but Winter's still stuck there, and I need to get back to Pye as fast as I can! You know how to adjust the mirrors, don't you?'

'Well . . .' Suuu looked hopefully at the sun, but her truth time wasn't over yet and she sighed. 'Yes.'

'Then set them for Pye's reality.'

Suuu hesitated. Then: 'What's it like where you've been?'

'What?' Angel was thrown by the question, and her temper frayed. 'Flackers, what does it matter what it's like? That child is *dangerous*, and she's got my friend, and—'

'Is your friend famous, then?' Suuu asked.

'No, for Tokyo's sake! Or at least, he was, sort of – we both were – but—' Then suddenly Angel's brain caught up with the rest of her and the explanation collapsed in a splutter. '*What's this got to do with anything?*' she yelled, so furiously that Suuu's horse backed a startled pace.

Suuu soothed the horse and shrugged. 'I wondered, that's all. Usually she only takes famous people. That's partly why she won't take me.'

'You mean, you *want* to go there?'

Suuu shrugged a second time. 'Well . . . I wouldn't mind seeing what it's like. All those games and roles sound like fun. And this place,' she waved a dismissive hand at the park in general, 'can get pretty boring.'

'You,' said Angel savagely, 'are completely and utterly

93

mad! And if you don't stop twisting my circuits and get those mirrors set for Pye's reality, then—'

'All right, all *right!*' Suuu interrupted huffily. 'There's no need to be *quite* so bad-tempered!' She swung one leg over the horse's saddle and slid to the ground. 'Hold Sometimes,' she said, shoving the reins into Angel's hand.

'What?'

'The horse. That's his name: Sometimes. Sometimes it is, anyway.' A feeble grin. 'My joke. Not very good, is it?' She vaulted the pool rim and sploshed to the fountain sculpture. 'Now, let's see . . . that one goes like this, and the one next to it like *this* . . .' Reflections danced across the pool's surface as she fiddled with the mirrors. Then: 'Right-o. That should get you back to Pye.'

Sometimes was nudging Angel, hoping she might have a titbit for him. She pushed his inquiring muzzle away and handed him back to Suuu as she returned. Suuu took the reins and said, 'Look . . .'

Angel paused with one leg half-over the pool rim. 'What now?' she growled.

'It might be an idea if I came back with you. To Pye's world.'

Angel stared at her. 'You have to be joking!'

'No, I'm not. And it's still my truth time, so I'm not lying, either. It's just that . . . I might be able to help. I know a few things about Tertia that could be useful. Pye won't be annoyed. I've visited him several times.' She glanced at Sometimes. 'We both have.' She saw Angel's surprised expression and smiled. 'He offered us a home, in fact . . . once.' Because I'm an Aberrant, and I don't really fit in here, he thought I'd prefer to live in his reality.' She patted Sometimes's nose. 'I like his world, but . . . well, I'm *used* to this one. And when it isn't my truth time I can cause a lot of trouble; I'd have driven Pye nuts after a while, so I turned the invitation down. But he always said, come again any time. So . . .' She shrugged and gave Angel a hopeful grin.

Angel wavered. She didn't want the responsibility of taking Suuu with her. But if she could throw any light on the problem of Tertia . . .

'All right,' she said. 'I'll take you.'

'*Yay!*' Suuu punched the air triumphantly. 'Come on, Sometimes!'

The horse trotted obediently towards the pool. 'You're not taking *him*?' Angel protested.

'Of course I am! I can't leave him behind on his own, can I? Someone might go off with him. Don't worry; he won't bite or kick on the way through. I told you, we've both done this before.'

Angel gave up. At the pool Suuu said '*Hup!*' and Sometimes jumped the rim wall, landing in the water with a splash that soaked Angel's entire front.

'Sorry!' Suuu waded cheerfully to the mirrors. Angel followed, dripping, and joined her at the fountain. They concentrated; light flared, and a horsy snort of surprise was the last thing Angel heard before the world of liars vanished.

## NINE

Pye was in his workshop, but he wasn't working. He was in fact taking a few mins off, and had just settled down in his favourite battered chair to enjoy some Tee when the mirrors of the matrix doorway started to flash and flicker. Pye scrambled eagerly to his feet – and a blast of light exploded blindingly through the room.

The arrival of two people and a fully grown horse in the cluttered workshop was spectacular to say the least. With a shrill whinny Sometimes took a flying leap out of the gateway, his hooves scattering objects right and left. He skidded on a threadbare rug and slid like a skater across the floor, with Suuu chasing after him. The two of them collided by the door; Suuu grabbed a wildly swinging rein and Sometimes swung round and stopped, snorting indignantly, with a trail of chaos in his wake.

Suuu said, 'Hello, Pye,' and from the gateway, where she had stepped through more decorously, Angel looked at the mess and added guiltily, 'Er . . . sorry.'

Hands on hips, Pye stared at them all. 'Please,' he said, '*don't* explain. Just tell me what you've found out.' His eyes narrowed. 'And where are Winter and Twinkle?'

Angel and Suuu both started talking at once, which made it impossible for Pye to understand anything. He waved his arms for silence, then glanced at Sometimes, who was looking uneasy and twitching his tail in a foreboding sort of way.

'*Not* in here, Suuu!' said Pye. 'Take him outside, please – you know the way.'

Suuu went red and hastily led Sometimes away, leaving Angel and Pye alone. 'Well?' Pye asked.

She told him the story. It was garbled, but Pye got the gist of it. And as he listened, his expression became very serious.

'Wait a sec.' He held up a hand as she started to describe the encounter in the Throne Chamber. 'This child – about ten years old, you say? Silver-blonde hair and freckles?'

'Yes; and she calls herself Queen, and she's got some sort of energy field that she controls, because when I wouldn't—'

'All right, all right, I'll hear about that in a min. Did she tell you her name?'

Angel nodded. 'She's called Tertia.'

Pye paled, and said hollowly, 'Oh, flackers . . .'

It was so unusual for him to swear in the language of Angel's world that she was completely thrown. Then she realised what his reaction implied, and her eyes widened. 'You *know* her?'

'I do. Or rather, did. A very long time ago.'

Angel frowned. 'But she's only—'

'Ten years old? She might look it, my dear, but I assure you, a hundred years would be more like the truth.'

Angel was trying to digest that statement when the door opened and Suuu returned, alone.

'It's all right,' she said. 'We made it to the garden before he – well, you know. It won't do your flowers any harm, anyway.' She beamed cheerfully. 'I've left him out there. Gregory says he'll get him some oats, so . . . Ah. Something's wrong, isn't it?'

'Yes,' said Pye. 'Something is.' He swung round and looked at Suuu. 'Is this one of your truth times?'

She nodded. 'Mind you, I don't know how long it'll last.'

'Then we'd better make the most of it while we can. Suuu, I know you've met this girl, Tertia. I want you to tell me *everything* you know about her.'

'Um,' said Suuu. 'Well . . . She's got a temper on her, I can promise you that. She calls it "getting cross", but if you ask me it's more like a one-girl war when she gets going. The first time we met, I annoyed her. I can't remember what I said but I was probably lying. She didn't like it, so she waggled her fingers and the next thing I knew I was wedged upside-down ten metres up a tree. Took me *ages* to get down.'

'She did something like that to me, too,' Angel put in. 'When I told her I wasn't going to play her games.'

'Bet you changed your mind after that,' said Suuu. They exchanged understanding looks.

'She's improved her skills, then,' Pye mused. 'And you said games . . . she's very keen on games, am I right?'

'Double-A!' Angel agreed with feeling. 'That whole *world* of hers is a game! It's like a huge ongoing Vee-fict; she gives all the people she's kidnapped roles to play, and if they don't play properly—'

'Queen Tertia gets cross,' supplied Suuu. 'Mind you, she

98

never stays cross for long. Take me: the second time I met her she'd forgotten all about our little spat and was sweet as bee-juice. I don't think she's got much of an attention span.'

'She hasn't; which is just about the only saving grace we have to work on.' Pye had started to pace, hands clasped twitchily behind his back. Angel knew that was his deep-thinking mode, so she said nothing else but waited for him to speak again.

At last he did. 'Angel. Do you really think that Winter and Twinkle will be all right for a while?'

She nodded. 'Winter's clicked in to her programme, and he's seen what she can do. He'll play along. And you know what Twinkle's like; provided somebody feeds her she'll stand on her head to please them.'

'Good. Then we have a little teeway – and I think we're going to need it, for planning and strategy.' Pye glanced at a clock on the wall and demanded, 'Time?'

The clock, which had no hands and was one of his more eccentric experiments, wheezed, and a mechanical voice replied, 'Bong . . . bong . . . bong . . . bong . . . bong . . . And seventeen minutes.'

'Right,' said Pye. 'First things first. Who's hungry?'

Though she hadn't thought about it amid everything else Angel was actually ravenous, and she nodded. Suuu did, too.

'Then we'll eat,' said Pye. 'Can't think or work properly on an empty stomach. Ring for Gregory, Angel. Over dinner I'll tell you the whole sorry story of 'Queen' Tertia and you'll understand what we're *really* up against.'

★  ★  ★

In the middle of dinner, Angel started crying. It was a reaction, Pye said, and perfectly natural. She'd had a few nasty experiences in Tertia's reality, and the confusion of meeting her mother again, coupled with fear for her and for Winter, was enough to set anyone off. The upset only lasted a few minutes, and afterwards Angel felt better, if a little foolish.

She also felt angry. And that, Pye told her, was a very good thing indeed.

'Bee-juice sweetness isn't going to get us anywhere with Tertia,' he said. 'Bees sting as well, remember. And that particular Queen Bee . . . Well, I'd better start at the beginning I suppose. Tertia is from my own reality. And she's the result of an experiment that went wrong.

'While I was still studying at University,' Pye went on, 'the elders – my tutors – were trying to find a way to stop people from ageing.' It was a dangerous idea, and they were going about it the wrong way, and I could have told them so; but I was much too young for them to take any notice of me. The first two efforts were an absolute disaster. But the third – to begin with, anyway – appeared to be more successful. A dear, pretty girl child, who appeared to grow up mentally yet physically stayed childlike. But they hadn't bargained for her personality.'

'Tertia?' said Angel.

'Exactly. The name has a link with the Latin for "three", and – oh, never mind; I imagine no one's ever *heard* of Latin where you come from. Where was I? Oh, yes – what the elders wanted was a human being who was normal in every way, except for the fact that they wouldn't age. What they got, however, was someone who wasn't normal in any way whatsoever. Tertia was *extremely* intelligent. Too intelligent for anyone's comfort, in fact. But she was also – and by the sound of it still is – cunning, vicious and thoroughly unpredictable. They couldn't teach her anything. Not because she wasn't able to learn, but because they simply couldn't get her to obey them. And when they tried to *force* her to obey, they found out that their tinkering had had some side effects.'

Tertia, it seemed, was telekinetic. All she had to do was concentrate hard enough, and she could control objects or people as though they were on invisible wires. The elders hadn't believed her abilities at first, but a few dramatic incidents had convinced them. Such as the time when they had locked her in her room for disobedience, and half an hour later had seen the entire building apparently taking itself to pieces, brick by brick, until all that was left was a pile of rubble with Tertia scarlet-faced and glowering triumphantly in the middle of the debris.

'That was an extreme example,' said Pye. 'She was exhausted by the effort and it took her several days to recover. But from then on the elders were very careful indeed. It wasn't "do this" and "do that" any more; it was "please, Tertia" and "thank you, Tertia". They were *scared* of her.'

'I'm not surprised,' said Angel. She didn't like the way this explanation was going. Clearly Tertia was even more dangerous that she had realised.

Suuu, who had also been listening with great interest,

said brightly, 'But I bet you weren't scared of her, were you, Pye?'

Pye sighed. 'You know me too well, Suuu. No, I wasn't. I felt sorry for Tertia. Long after I'd discovered my mirror doorways and left my world for this reality, I couldn't stop thinking about her. The way the elders treated her was an insult to any intelligent creature, and, silly fool that I am, I wanted to help her. So one night – oh, *years* later – I went back to my old world, and I invited her to come and live with me.'

'Whoo!' said Suuu.

'Indeed: whoo! It was a *very* big mistake. I thought that the treatment she was given was the cause of her viciousness, and once she was here she would settle down and become a nicer person. Dear me, was I wrong! It was mayhem right from the start – she was rude, disruptive, destructive, and the more I tried to be kind to her, the more she seemed to enjoy causing trouble.

In the end, I simply couldn't stand it any longer. I admitted defeat, and sent Tertia back to her own reality. She wasn't the least bit reluctant to go: in fact her last words to me were that I was a boring old man, living in a boring old dump, where the games were boring, and everything was boring, and if she never set eyes on my boring face again it would be too soon. I must say, I breathed a sigh of relief when she stepped through the gateway and left my reality for good.

But now, years later, it seems my kindness has finally backfired on me. Tertia looks and acts like a child, but she is also extremely clever. She obviously learned a lot while she was staying with me – she was forever poking and prying in my workshop but I never thought she would learn anything of any use. I was wrong. What Tertia learned was very useful indeed. It enabled her to unravel the secret of the mirror doorways.

'She must have spent years experimenting and exploring, until she found an uninhabited reality that she liked,' Pye continued grimly. 'Then all she had to do was move in, set herself up as Queen – she used to love pretending to be a Queen – and start kidnapping people to play her courtiers.'

'Soho thinks she's in Vee,' Angel added, her face miserable. 'She kept talking about her agent and her salary. She really believes she's been contracted to act in a fict, and Tertia's the main star, or the producer's daughter, or something.'

Privately, Pye thought Soho was a very foolish woman, and her behaviour didn't surprise him in the least. 'It's probably just as well,' he reassured Angel. 'It'll stop her from panicking. And it might also be helpful to us . . .'

'What do you mean?'

'Games, my dear Angel, games. They are Tertia's greatest delight, and fict-acting is a game, after all.' Pye's face had brightened somewhat. 'I think it's time for a little planning, and Soho might prove very useful.' He eyed Suuu sidelong. 'As might one or two other people who come to mind . . .'

'Me?' said Suuu, pointing to herself. 'Ooh, yes please! Especially if it means I get to go there!'

'You will. Quite soon, in fact, if the idea I have brewing

works out. Now: have we all had enough to eat?' He scanned the table. There were some leftovers, but of course Twinkle wasn't there. 'Good. Then Gregory can clear away – and we can get down to work.'

The vital thing, Pye declared, was information. In particular he wanted to see what Winter had recorded on the gizmos he had been given. Yes, he knew Angel had taken gizmos, too, but he'd looked at what was on them and – 'without wishing to be rude, my dear' – she hadn't actually *used* them much, had she? Winter was . . . well, let's say he was more *interested* in technology. He would have made readings of just about everything; was probably still doing so, in fact. So the first priority was to retrieve the devices he had. Which, naturally, meant that someone must return to Tertia's play-world.

'I can't take the risk of going myself,' Pye said. 'If Tertia sets eyes on me she will know immediately that she is in for trouble, and we certainly don't want to alert her at this stage. From what you've told me, Angel, I don't think she'll "get cross" if you show up again; she simply isn't interested in you. But someone will have to distract her for the time it takes you to see Winter. That's where Suuu can be useful, so she can go with you – and it'll satisfy her curiosity, eh, Suuu?'

'What curiosity?' said Suuu.

She hadn't spoken for some while, and when they both looked at her they saw that there was a peculiar frown on her face.

'Tertia's world,' Angel prompted. 'You want to see it.'

Suuu blinked. 'No, I don't think so. Do I? Probably not.' She squeezed her eyes shut. '*Oww* . . . oh, I wish my head would stop *doing* this . . .'

'Uh-oh. . .' said Pye. 'I suspect she's—'

He was interrupted as Suuu's eyes opened again and she grinned at them. 'Whose world?' she said. 'Never heard of it. Never heard of her, either. Or him. Or it. Or you, for that matter.'

'Oh, hell's bells!' Pye growled. 'That's *just* what we need! Your timing, Suuu, is atrocious! Still, I suppose you don't have any control over it, so—'

'Yes, I do. I can control absolutely anything and everything. Oh, by the way, if you see an animal that doesn't look like a horse hanging around here, it's not mine.'

Pye sighed heavily. 'This is a gargantuan nuisance! If we wait for her next truth time before you go to retrieve Winter's devices, we could be twiddling our thumbs for a week!'

'But do we *have* to wait?' said Angel. 'You wanted her to be a distraction for Tertia. It seems to me that distractions don't come much better than Suuu in this mode!'

'You've got a point there . . . yes, it makes sense. You'll have to remember not to misunderstand anything she says or does, but if you're careful . . .'

Angel smiled dryly. 'I might not be much good at technology, but Suuu isn't technology. She's people.'

'No, I'm not,' Suuu corrected her cheerfully. 'I'm a fieldmouse. You know; one of those green things, about five metres tall, with feathers and—'

Pye said, 'Keep talking, Suuu,' and Suuu instantly shut up. 'There you see,' Pye told Angel. 'She isn't that difficult to handle. It's all a matter of interpretation: whatever you want her to do, tell her the opposite, and she'll be as good as gold.'

Angel nodded. 'I'll manage. Anyway, we shouldn't be gone long.' She paused. 'What about Sometimes?'

'He can stay here. Poor fellow: Suuu usually gives him a new coat of paint when she goes into untruth mode, so he'll probably be glad of the respite. Now, Suuu . . .' raising his voice, 'I'm going to ask you *not* to do something.'

Suuu gave him a suspicious look. 'I might want to do it.'

'No, you won't, and you can't anyway. Angel isn't going to Tertia's reality, and you can't go with her.'

Suuu's eyes lit up like beacons. '*Yay!*' she yelped triumphantly. 'When don't we leave?'

## TEN

Something was different. Angel knew it as soon as she stepped through the gateway into New Players' Reception; for the first few secs she thought it was a feeling in the air, but then she realised it was more tangible than that. To start with, there was the smell. It was sharp and acrid, reminding her of her time in Winter's reality, and after a quick surf through her memory she placed it. Burned wood, with something else, unfamiliar, mixed in. Then there was the light in the room. When she left, it had been bright almost to glaring point, but now it had sunk to a dull, sullen glow, as if something had gone very wrong with the power systems.

The mirrors flickered again as Suuu emerged after her. Suuu stared, assessing their surroundings, then said, 'This isn't exciting.'

'No, it isn't,' Angel agreed. *But it could get exciting: too exciting, if my instincts are right. . .* 'Come on,' she added, then remembering Suuu's state of mind, 'or rather, don't. I'm not going to find Winter.'

She opened the door and peered cautiously into the passage outside. No one around; no sound from anywhere, either, which might or might not be a good sign. The Throne Chamber was . . . *that* way.

She set off, with Suuu at her heels.

The Throne Chamber wasn't that way. Instead, Angel opened another door and found herself emerging into the garden, with its dizzying drop and vast view of the sky and sea. It was getting towards dusk – which she thought might explain the light – and the acrid smell was suddenly stronger. Very strong, in fact. And there were black smuts blowing on the breeze, fluttering downwards from somewhere above and to her right . . .

Angel looked up. Above her was what had been a cluster of ridiculous and rickety turrets sticking at precarious angles from the main bulk of the castle. But someone had set fire to them recently by the look of it, and all that was left was a tattered mess of ragged cardboard edges, gaping paper holes, blackened and broken wooden struts, with smoke still drifting in the sky behind them.

'Tokyo!' Angel's eyes widened in alarm. Another small rain of ashes eddied down, and she batted them away, still staring.

Then from high up a petulant voice yelled out.

'I *said*, I want a *technician!*' It was, unmistakably, Tertia. Another voice mumbled something in reply, and Tertia screeched, 'Well, you'll have to *be* one! And fix it properly, because if it goes wrong again I'll do something even *worse!*'

Suuu raised her eyebrows. 'I don't know that voice,' she said. 'And it's certainly nothing to worry about.'

Angel took no notice of her. By the sound of it Tertia was somewhere in, or at least near, the burned towers. Which meant that, if Winter was still installed as Pretend Handsome Prince, it should be possible to get to him, get the gizmos and be back in Pye's workshop without her being any the wiser.

'Stay here,' she told Suuu, to make her follow. They set off back into the castle. *Should have turned left instead of right at that last but one corridor . . .* ah, this was it; she could see the tacky doors of the Throne Chamber ahead.

'Right.' She glanced at Suuu. 'We're not going in quietly, we're going to crash straight through and make as much noise as we can.'

'Absolutely,' said Suuu, and started to tiptoe. Angel put her ear to the doors, listening. No sound from inside . . . or was there? A sort of squeaking; almost, but not quite, like singing . . . A smile spread over her face as she recognised the noise.

'*I'm just a little Funfriend, Funfriend, Funfriend . . .*' It was one of Twinkle's favourites; it had nineteen verses and was guaranteed to drive anyone demented after six or seven, but Twinkle only sang it when she was happy.

Angel pushed open the doors and eased into the Throne Chamber.

Winter was there, and when she saw him she struggled not to laugh out loud. His Handsome Prince outfit consisted of baggy trousers made from a papery, glitter-stripe material, a lurid purple furry shirt several sizes too big for him, and an enormous gold ruff around his neck that stuck out at a stiff angle, making his head look as if it was presented on an oversized plate. Topping the lot was Soho's crown with its metre-high spikes. He looked a complete *earwig* and Angel spluttered hilariously.

Winter saw her and scowled. 'All right, I know! Ha, ha!'

Twinkle's singing (which seemed to be coming from under the Throne) stopped, and Angel sobered up. 'Sorry.'

'Me, too,' Suuu added, and sniggered loudly.

Winter stared at her. 'What in the stars is *she* doing here?'

'Who?' Suuu looked over her shoulder and probably would have said something ridiculous, but Angel interrupted quickly.

'I'll explain later; but take no notice of her, she's in telling-lies mode.' She jerked her head in the approximate direction of the burned turrets. 'What happened up there?'

'I'm not sure,' Winter said, though he still eyed Suuu warily. 'I *think* something short-circuited in the electronic systems and caught fire inside the wall. The first I knew about it was when someone came piling in here gabbling that the whole court was going up in flames. It wasn't, of course, but Tertia started screaming for someone to sort it. The soldiers put it out, but then she yelled that she wanted a technician to fix the circuits, and when there wasn't one, she had a complete fit and started using that energy to throw things – and people – around.'

'She still is,' said Angel. 'We heard her. Look, Winter, we're not here to stay. We've been back to Pye, and he needs the recording devices you brought with you.'

'Fine.' Winter fished under his clothes. 'I've kept them hidden, and I've been taking more readings.' He scowled. 'I told her I could fix those blown circuits, but apparently Handsome Princes aren't allowed to do things like that.'

He handed the gizmos over, and as he did so there was

a kerfuffle under the Throne and Twinkle emerged. She was wearing a little coat in the same ghastly furry purple as Winter's shirt, and she looked smug and fatter.

'Hello, Angel!' she said brightly. 'I like it here. I've had *lots* of food. Sweeties, and ice cream, and some fishy stuff, and—'

'Not now, Twinkle!' Angel looked at Winter. 'Can you two hold on a bit longer, while Pye makes some plans?'

'Sure.' Winter nodded. 'I know how to stay out of trouble, and Tertia's taken a huge liking to Twinkle. We'll be fine.'

'That's a relief! And – what about Soho?'

'Don't worry, she's all right. Tertia's forgotten all about the gardening and given her a new role to play.' Winter grimaced. 'Soho still thinks this whole thing's a Vee-fict. I'm almost beginning to believe it myself . . .'

'Don't believe it, whatever you do!' Angel warned him. 'There's a lot you don't know yet. Pye's encountered Tertia before, and after what he told me, I promise you she's *got* to be stopped, fast. I can't go into it now, because Pye says we daren't waste any time, but I'll get back as soon as I can, and—'

'Aha!'

The voice from the doorway made everyone jump. Angel swung round – and there was Tertia.

'You're the technician!' she declared, striding forward and pointing at Angel.

'What?' Angel was horrified. 'No I'm not, I'm—'

'You are, because I *say* you are! You've got just the right costume, anyway, so you're not allowed not to be! All the lights in the South Wing have gone wrong, so get over there and technish! Now!'

Before Angel could think of any kind of reply, Suuu spoke up. 'Good morning!' she said. 'We've never met. My name's Elori, and I *always* tell the truth.'

Tertia glowered at her, and a glimmer of uncertainty showed on her face. 'I know you from somewhere . . . Are you famous?'

'Oh, *absolutely*! Much more famous than everyone else here. And I can technish, too; in fact I'm better at it than anyone you've ever seen.'

'You are, are you? Good! Then go and fix the lights.' Tertia's bright, cold little eyes swivelled round to Angel again. 'You're not a technician any more. I'll find something else for you. Give your equipment to *her*.'

*Equipment*? Angel thought, baffled. Then she saw where Tertia's eyes had focused. Winter's recording devices. She'd forgotten to hide them.

She began in desperation, 'Er – no, wait; these aren't—'

'*Yes they are!*' Tertia snarled. 'Give them to the technician! *Now*!!'

Knowing what Tertia could do if she wasn't obeyed, Angel had no choice. Maybe if she went with Suuu she could grab them back once they were out of Tertia's sight—

'Where do you think you're going?' Tertia snapped as Suuu set off and Angel started to follow.

'I – um – I'm her assistant. I'm going along to help.'

'She isn't allowed to have any assistants,' Tertia declared. 'We're going to play something else.'

'Hello,' said Suuu from the door, and waved. 'I'm not going now.'

Angel flung a frantic look at Winter. He got the message and called out, 'Thank you, technician. Whatever you do, you won't take those devices back to the workshop where you came from, will you?'

'No way!' Suuu promised cheerily, and went.

Would she go back to Pye? Angel prayed she would, but she knew it was a slim chance—

'Right!' Tertia's shout and a sharp clapping of hands made Angel jump, and quickly she pushed her worries away.

'I'm bored with all these games!' Tertia announced. 'I'm going to think of some new ones.' She paced across the Throne Chamber, one finger tapping her chin thoughtfully, then abruptly stopped and turned to face Winter. 'You're the Handsome Prince but you don't *do* much. Handsome Princes are supposed to *do* things. You!' to Angel. 'Tell me something that Handsome Princes are supposed to do.'

'What?' Angel was flummoxed. 'I don't know!'

'You've got to know! I say so! Come on – tell me!'

Frantically Angel scrabbled around in her memory, and suddenly recalled Avalonne, her own fantasy Vee world. Grabbing the first Avalonne adventure that came into her head, she said, 'They rescue people.'

'Hmm.' Tertia started to look interested. 'What sort of people, and what from?'

'Well . . . damsels in distress, usually. The damsels have been captured by wicked sorcerers, or dragons, and they get shut up in a tower and the princes have to brave all kinds of perils to rescue them . . .' Angel was so anxious to avoid angering Tertia that she didn't think through the implications of what she was saying. Only when she saw the look of horror coming over Winter's face did she realise what she had done.

'Braving perils . . .' Tertia mused. 'Mmm. I *like* that. The damsel is a prisoner, and he,' jerking a thumb in Winter's direction, 'has got to face danger to rescue her. If he doesn't do it in time, or makes a mistake, they both get killed or eaten—'

'Hover!' Angel protested. 'I didn't mean anything like that—'

'Shut up, *I'm* talking. But if he wins, then they have a banquet and all live happily ever after.'

Twinkle's ears pricked up. 'Banquet? Yum! Can we play banquets now?'

Tertia looked fondly at the Therapet and her voice turned downright syrupy. 'Soon. He's got to rescue the damsel first, though.'

'Your Majesty . . .' Winter ventured. His face had turned pale. 'What – um – sort of dangers will I have to face?'

Tertia's smile was horrible. 'I haven't decided yet, but I'll think of plenty. Now, you're the Handsome Prince who does the rescuing, and *you*,' pointing at Angel, 'are going to be the damsel he rescues. Or who gets killed and eaten, if he fails in his quest.'

'But—'

'*Shut up!* And *I'll* be the evil sorceress, who takes the

damsel prisoner.' She positively leered now. 'This game is going to be fun!'

Twinkle, oblivious to the increasingly ominous mood, asked, 'Can I play?'

'Of course you can,' Tertia assured her. 'But you're not the Handsome Prince's Magic Cat any more. You're the Evil Sorceress's Magic Cat, instead. That means you come with me, and you do Magic.'

'Magic some more nice food?' Twinkle suggested.

'Oh, we'll find something better than that.' Tertia had a maniacal smirk on her face by this time. 'Right. I want courtiers, I want soldiers, and I want lots of extras to make the game busy and exciting. And you can all have costumes.' She pointed at Winter. 'Call the servants, Handsome Prince. Let's get *moving*!'

Angel guessed it must be nearly midnight, but her mind was in such a spin that she could no longer be sure of anything. All she could focus on clearly was the certain knowledge that Tertia was seriously and dangerously mad.

There must be forty or fifty people involved now in the new 'game'. Tertia had gone shrieking and stamping and threatening round the castle, rounding up everyone she could find, until she had a bewildered crowd mustered in the Throne Chamber to be assigned their roles in the drama of the Handsome Prince and the Damsel In Distress. Soho had been one of the first to arrive, and was very piqued that 'a little nobody who hasn't even *been* here five mins!' had been given the Damsel's role. One menacing look from Tertia had stopped her complaints, but she had continued to sulk and glower at Angel.

Angel would gladly have traded places with her. Being in the clutches of Tertia at all was bad enough, but Tertia as 'evil sorceress' was a truly horrifying prospect. Tertia had wasted no time in dressing the part; flowing robes with glitter-black wings that made her look like an outsize bat; an ornate black and silver mask that hid most of her face . . . and her Magic Sword. The sword, naturally, wasn't magic – but it wasn't cardboard, either. Angel had found that out when one of Tertia's soldiers had failed to obey an order quickly enough and she had taken a swipe at him. She'd missed – but the blade had cut straight through a cardboard pillar as if it was made of glitter-ice. Everyone had been *very* obedient after that.

And now Angel was climbing a spiral staircase that seemed to go on for ever. The stairs were wooden and rickety, and normally nothing on earth would have persuaded her to go near them. But Tertia was a metre behind her and the sword blade was pointed at her back; so Angel climbed.

Tertia was thoroughly involved in her part now, muttering incantations as she went and occasionally crying, '*Hahaaar!*' or cackling dementedly in full Evil Sorceress mode. Angel had been 'captured' and they were going, apparently, to her Lair in a high tower, where the Damsel in Distress was supposed to plead for mercy, fail to get it, and be left wringing her hands as she waited for the Handsome Prince to come galloping to the rescue. In many ways the plot was just like the scenarios Angel had invented for herself in Vee-Avalonne. The only differences

116

were that, in Avalonne, Angel Ravenhair was always the rescuer rather than the victim; and in Vee, if someone did something gruesome to someone else, it didn't actually *hurt*.

To top it all, Twinkle was now happily installed as the Evil Sorceress's Magic Cat. The Therapet had no idea of the real danger; to her, the whole thing was simply a huge, harmless and fun game. She balanced now on Tertia's shoulder, eyes huge with excitement, tail waving, occasionally chipping in her own '*Hahaaar*'s or gurgling growls to add to the atmosphere.

And it certainly was atmospheric. Angel was much too preoccupied to worry about the actual time, but it had been pitch dark outside for ages, and the occasional light panels on the staircase walls didn't help much. It was also raining heavily. The noise of water hammering on the castle's flimsy fabric spooked Angel badly, and once or twice she was sure she had heard thunder rumbling ominously in the distance. A full-blown storm was *all* she needed: the perfect shiver-fict background to send her nerves right off the scale.

The spiral stairs ended suddenly, as Angel came face to face with a door. It looked heavy and grim, with enormous hinges and a grille in the middle just large enough for someone to peer through.

'Hahaaar!' cried Tertia. 'Your prison, damsel!' She shoved past Angel, waving the sword perilously, and with a dramatic gesture flung the door open. 'Get in there!'

The door wobbled back on its hinges, and one stunningly simple fact smacked into Angel's mind. For all its appearance, the door was as flimsy as everything else in this insane place. Thin wood, cardboard, paper, paint. From a distance it had looked so convincing. But in reality, the moment Tertia was gone it would be the easiest thing in the world to punch a fist through it and walk straight out.

Angel's spirits soared, and only a quick jolt of common sense stopped her from grinning as maniacally as Tertia. Twinkle said, 'Grrr!' and Tertia aimed a whack at Angel with (thankfully) the flat of the sword blade.

'I said, get *in*! Play properly, or I'll *do* something!'

Angel snapped to her senses. She was no actress, but she waved her arms around and said, 'Help!' and 'Mercy!' Tertia prodded her through the door, then pulled a wonky lever just inside. There was a sputtering noise inside the wall, and a couple of dim lights came on, allowing Angel to see the Lair.

It didn't look much like a prison. Admittedly the single window was tiny and had bars, but the only other object here, if you ignored the dust and cobwebs, was a cylindrical metal shaft that came up through the floor and disappeared into the ceiling. Angel couldn't imagine what it was for – unless the idea was to hold the tower together. It certainly needed holding; plaster had fallen off the walls, leaving large, damp patches, and the ceiling was shored up with lengths of wood. And it smelled revolting.

There was a blue flicker beyond the window, followed by a far off noise that definitely *was* thunder. 'Oh, *good*!' said Tertia gleefully. 'There *is* going to be a storm. That makes it even more fun!'

'Mercy!' Angel repeated, trying to get into the spirit of the thing.

Tertia leered at her. 'No mercy for you, Damsel!' She whipped a length of cord from the folds of her costume. 'Now, stand still while I tie you up!'

'*What*?' Angel hadn't bargained for that. 'No, wait, you can't—'

'*Yes I can*!' Tertia's face twisted. She threw the sword aside and made a sharp gesture, and Angel shot a metre into the air.

Tertia smiled. She pointed, then moved her pointing finger towards the metal shaft. Angel felt herself move, and there wasn't a thing she could do about it. She bumped gently against the shaft, then slid slowly down with her back against it, until she was within Tertia's reach.

'Stop kicking!' Tertia ordered. She was coiling the cord in her hands. It was a long cord, and when she wound it around Angel, it bound her against the shaft from her armpits to her knees.

'There!' Tertia stepped back and surveyed her handiwork with great satisfaction. 'Now you wait here for the Handsome Prince to rescue you!'

Angel gave an experimental wriggle, but the cord and the shaft held firm. *Oh, Tokyo*! she thought. *I'll never get out of this without help*!

Tertia snatched up her sword and strode towards the door, then stopped and looked back, her expression sly. 'There's something the Handsome Prince doesn't know,' she said. 'I'm not going to tell him, but I'll tell you. That metal rod you're tied to. Do you know what it's for?' Angel

119

shook her head uneasily, and Tertia giggled. 'It's for when there's a storm. This place is high up, and it could easily get hit by lightning. The rod's here to attract the lightning and channel it away, so that nothing else gets damaged.' She waggled the sword almost playfully in Angel's direction. 'If this storm comes overhead and lightning *does* strike, there'll be an *enormous* flash . . . and not much left of you. So you'd better hope the Handsome Prince gets here quickly, hadn't you? Bye bye, Damsel.'

She went out, and in a daze of frozen terror Angel heard her cackling theatrically away down the stairs.

# ELEVEN

Angel shut her eyes tightly and counted the secs following the flash. Four . . . five . . . six . . .

*Rrrrumble . . .*

It wasn't here yet, but it was definitely getting closer. And worse. The thunder seemed to echo on for mins, and the unsteady lights had dipped alarmingly just now. The storm was stalking towards her, and the rain on the tower roof was like threatening drums, and Winter hadn't come, and she couldn't get free, and she was totally and hideously *frightened*.

Where was Winter? He was supposed to be the Handsome Prince rushing to the rescue – surely he must get here soon? *Unless Tertia's done something dreadful, and he won't come at all . . .*

She frantically shoved that idea out of her head and strained, yet again, against the cords. They didn't budge a centi: Tokyo alone knew what they must be made of. If only she had a knife—

From behind her, something announced, 'Grrr!'

Angel froze rigid, and her eyes opened like saucers as Twinkle trotted into her view. Twinkle stretched, yawned, then blinked at her.

'Hello, Angel.'

Angel's heart gave a gigantic leap. '*Twinkle*! How

in the stars did you get in here?'

'I haven't been anywhere,' Twinkle said. 'I'm on guard. I'm the Evil Sorceress's Magic Cat, and I've got to make sure the Damsel doesn't escape.' She yawned again. 'I had a *lovely* sleep.'

'Twinkle, you've got to help me! Use your teeth to chew through the cords!'

'Why?' Twinkle wanted to know.

Another flicker of lightning lit up the window, and the wall lights made an unpleasant electrical noise. 'Because I've got to get out!' Angel told her. 'Twinkle, *please!*'

Twinkle went cross-eyed, the way she always did when she was thinking about something more difficult than food. Then: 'Shan't. It's Not Allowed.'

'It *is* allowed!' Angel pleaded. 'The Evil Sorceress said so!'

'I didn't hear her. I'm on guard. Grrr! This is fun!'

'It's going to be anything but fun if lightning hits this tower!' Angel yelled. 'Lightning's very, very dangerous, and it'll *hurt!*'

'Won't,' said Twinkle. 'It's pretend.'

Angel realised that she wouldn't get anywhere. Twinkle believed this was all a fun game, and until and unless something nasty actually happened, she couldn't be made to understand the danger. The only hope was to try another tactic. And with Twinkle, only was one foolproof.

'Twinkle,' she said, 'Winter told me a secret.'

The little cat's eyes lit up. She loved secrets, even though she was hopeless at keeping them. 'What is it?' she wanted to know.

'Well, I shouldn't tell you really, but . . . when he comes to play the game with us, he's going to bring some ice cream.'

'Ooh!' said Twinkle. 'Really?'

'Really. He promised. The only thing is, I'm afraid he might forget.'

Twinkle looked appalled. 'Forget? He mustn't forget!'

'He might, though, unless somebody reminds him. I can't go and find him, because I'm tied up. But if you chewed the cords . . .' She smiled encouragingly.

Twinkle's ears flattened against her head, and she hesitated. Then: 'Mustn't!'

*Oh, flackers, it wasn't going to work, and there wasn't time to argue . . .* 'Well look,' Angel amended desperately, 'why don't you go and find him for me?'

'Not *supposed* to . . .' But Twinkle was wavering now.

'I know. But what if he forgets the ice cream?'

It worked. The thought of missing out on ice cream was stronger than anything Tertia could command, and Twinkle nodded. 'All right, then. He mustn't forget, must he? Ice cream's important!'

'Yes, it's very important. Go on then, hurry! And tell Winter . . .' Angel thought fast. 'Tell him that I'm going to be hit by lightning if he doesn't rescue me soon!'

Twinkle purred approvingly. 'That's a good game! I'll tell him.'

She had learned enough about the castle not to bother trying to open the door. One firm head–butt and a hole appeared in the cardboard. Twinkle vanished.

The next clap of thunder was a great deal closer.

'I don't *care* how much you want to start rescuing!' Tertia shrieked, stamping her foot. 'I'm the Queen, everyone has to do as I say, and I say the Handsome Prince rides a horse!'

'But, Your Majesty, there aren't any horses,' a Pretend Soldier whined ingratiatingly. 'Honestly, Your Majesty, we've looked everywhere!'

'*Then look again until you find one!*'

The soldier flinched as though someone had punched him, and no one in the Throne Chamber would meet anyone else's eyes. Soho was in a corner and seemed as if she was trying to dig a hole in the wall and hide in it; the rest just looked blankly into space with fixed smiles on their faces.

Tertia, purple in the face and breathing like a steam engine, stomped round in a circle. 'If someone doesn't bring the Handsome Prince a horse in the next five minutes,' she said ominously, 'then I am going to *do* something. And what I do will not be *nice*. *Do you understand*?'

There were murmurs of 'Yes, Your Majesty,' and 'Absolutely,' but nobody moved a muscle. On the Throne, where he had been sitting since Tertia told him not to move Or Else, Winter fidgeted restlessly, racking his brain for an answer to this newest dilemma. He had no idea what had become of Angel, but a sinister hint that 'even if you find her, it might be too late' had scared him badly. He had an awful feeling that Tertia really wanted to see someone get hurt. If that was so, then the 'game' had taken on a new and very unpleasant dimension, and her sudden demand for a horse that didn't exist was an obvious ploy to slow him down and weight the odds against Angel.

Tertia had started to count out loud, which was another way of intimidating people. She had got to thirty-four, and still no one had moved, when a little voice called from the doorway.

'Hello, everybody!'

Twinkle trotted in, tail up like a flagpole. Tertia saw her and tensed. 'What are you doing here? I told you to stay with the Damsel!'

Twinkle blinked happily at her. 'Got a message,' she said self-importantly, and headed towards Winter. 'Angel says you mustn't forget the ice cream. And . . .' She concentrated hard. 'Ooh, yes. And she says she'll get hit by lightning if you don't rescue her soon.'

'*What?*' Winter sprang to his feet. 'Twinkle, where is she? You've got to tell me!'

'She's in the—'

'*Shut up, you stupid animal!*' Tertia shrieked.

'—biggest tower, right at the top, and she's tied to a—'

Twinkle didn't get any further, for Tertia gave a wordless yell of rage. Her hand came up in a fast, twisting movement, and the little Therapet was hoicked off her feet to hang dangling helplessly somewhere near the ceiling.

'Ooooh!' Twinkle wailed, paddling the air, her fur standing on end. 'Put me down! Pleeeease!'

'*Stupid, brainless, disobedient creature!*' Tertia screamed. '*Disobedience is NOT ALLOWED!*'

Her hand drew back as if to hurl something. Winter shouted, 'No! Don't!' but he might as well have saved his breath. The force of Tertia's energy spun Twinkle around; she rotated faster and faster, howling in fright – then with no warning she spun away and hurtled across the Throne Chamber. She hit the wall with an enormous impact and crashed to the floor, where she lay motionless.

Winter was so shocked and horrified that he couldn't do anything but stare numbly at the pitiful furry heap by the wall. Then one of Twinkle's paws twitched. She raised her head groggily, staggered to her feet, and said in a small, bewildered voice, '*Hurt* me . . .'

'Twinkle!' Winter jumped from the Throne plinth and ran towards her. Tertia shouted, 'Leave the cat alone! Don't you *dare* touch it!' but fury and concern for Twinkle overrode Winter's fear. That was a mistake. The telekinetic force hit him when he was still three metres from Twinkle, and it knocked him backwards, scooping his feet from under him and bowling him over and over until he fetched up hard against the plinth again.

'I don't think you heard me properly,' Tertia hissed savagely, stalking towards him. 'I said, disobedience is *NOT ALLOWED* . . .'

Winter tried to sit up but found he couldn't. Something invisible was holding him as surely as if he'd been nailed to the floorboards, and the only part of him that would move was his head. He looked up into Tertia's demented eyes, and what he saw there made him quail.

Twinkle had stopped halfway to him. She was wobbly

on her feet but there didn't seem to be anything broken. She too looked at Tertia.

'Don't like this game any more . . .' she said unhappily.

Winter found his voice, though it came out as a croak. 'It isn't a game, Twinkle. Angel's in trouble . . . she needs help . . . *uhh!*' Tertia had launched another surge of energy that slammed his head against the plinth and left him sick and giddy, but he rallied against it. 'Help her, Twinkle! Help Angel!'

He heard a scuttering of paws, and Tertia whipped round. '*No*! Come back *here*!'

A voice squealed, '*Shan't! Pooey!*' and the force controlling Winter relaxed momentarily – enough for him to raise his head and see Twinkle bolting like a rabbit out of the door. Tertia's yell of frustration told him that her attempt to stop the Therapet had failed; and like a bolt from the lightning outside a realisation crashed into Winter's brain. *She wasn't able to—*

At that instant every thought was eclipsed by an almighty crashing and banging from somewhere in the depths of the castle.

Everyone froze, even Tertia. 'What,' she said, 'was *that*?'

A few people muttered fawning answers that meant nothing at all, and a voice that could only have one source quavered, 'I shall have an Episode, I just *know* I shall!' Tertia ignored them all. With a jolt that rattled his teeth she cast off her kinetic hold on Winter and strode for the door, bawling, '*Where are my soldiers? Fetch my army AT ONCE!*'

Then Winter heard the new noise. At first he didn't believe it, but after a sec or two he knew he couldn't be mistaken. In his home reality he had learned a lot about horses, and the noise was, indisputably, the clop and clatter of a horse's hooves. A *horse, here*? It wasn't *possible*—

It was possible. As Tertia reached the Throne Chamber door, a large shape loomed out of the murky half-light beyond. It was moving fast; so fast that Tertia had no time to yell 'Stop!', let alone do anything else. She jumped out of the way a bare fraction of a sec before Sometimes, with Suuu Beeen Aaat perched on his back and shouting 'Whoa!' came barrelling into the room.

At the sight of the crowd in the Throne Chamber, Sometimes did a double-take and slewed to a chaotic halt that nearly tipped Suuu off into Tertia's lap. Grabbing his mane and righting herself, she said breathlessly, 'Sorry! He gets over-excited when we make a reality jump.' She grinned at the assembly. 'Whoo! That's better. Hi, everyone. Have I missed much?'

Twinkle's circuits had been joggled by Tertia's attack, and she lost her way several times before she finally found the spiral staircase.

She was feeling very sorry for herself – but she had also recovered from the worst of her fright, and on its heels came indignation. She couldn't understand why the nice Queen person had suddenly turned on her, but whatever the reason, it wasn't *fair*. This game should have been fun, but the Queen person was spoiling it. She had shouted and done horrible things; there wasn't any ice cream, and she had hurt Twinkle, and she wouldn't let Winter rescue Angel. She was cheating. All right, then: Twinkle would rescue Angel, and if the Queen person didn't like it, she'd *bite* her and see what she thought of that!

The stairs were hard work for a little creature, but Twinkle pressed on. There was a lot of flashing and noise outside now; it was called a thunderstorm, and Twinkle didn't like thunderstorms. At home (she now thought of Pye's workshop as home) she always hid when one started, and didn't come out until someone promised that it had stopped. Now though, there wasn't anywhere to hide. Maybe Angel would know of a good place . . .

The whole world seemed to be made of eerily dancing blue light, and the higher she climbed, the louder the thunder's roar became. Twinkle was relieved at last to see the door to the tower room, and she wriggled through the hole she had made earlier.

As she entered, the thunderbolt exploded almost directly overhead. A blinding flash blotted out everything, and the entire tower shook to a colossal din like a mountain collapsing. Through it, Twinkle heard a shrill scream, and she charged forward.

'A-a-ange-e-el!' The shaking of the tower made her cry shake, too. Then the glare was gone, though the roar continued, and she saw Angel struggling against the cords.

'Angel?'

'Get these spidering things off me, *quickly*!' Angel shouted. 'That bolt must have missed by centis; I felt it in my *bones*!'

Twinkle pounced on the cords and began to gnaw. They were tough, but her teeth were tougher, they whirred like saw blades and within secs the cords snapped. Angel scrambled to her feet, then collapsed as cramp stabbed through her. Twinkle jumped around on her legs, making soothing noises, but Angel pushed her aside.

'Never mind that! What's – *ow*! – going on? Where's Winter?'

'Throne place,' said Twinkle. 'That Queen person was nasty, and she hurt me, and there isn't any ice cream. I ran away.' She paused. 'There was a big noise down there just afterwards.'

'Big noise? What sort of big noise?'

'Don't know. Didn't wait to see. I don't want to play this game any more!'

Angel paused in her panic. She stroked the Therapet's head. 'Neither do I. But Tertia – the Queen person – does, so we've got to find a way to stop her. I think . . .' Cautiously she tried standing up, and found that she could. 'I think we'd better go and look for Winter. Come on. But whatever happens, we mustn't let the Queen person see us, all right?'

Twinkle nodded. 'Don't want to see *her*, anyway!'

They headed for the spiral stairs.

'Of course he's a horse,' Suuu said huffily. 'But you can't have him. He's mine.'

Tertia glared from Suuu to Sometimes and back to Suuu again. 'I don't think you *quite* understand,' she said. 'I'm Queen here, and everyone has to—'

'Do as you say; yes, I heard you the first time.' Suuu was well aware of Winter making frantic warning gestures behind Tertia; she ignored them. 'But you see, where I come from, we don't have Queens. So I'm not used to taking orders from them. And I'm not going to take orders from you. In fact,' now she flashed a broad and very obvious conspiratorial grin at Winter, 'you can spider off.'

Tertia's face turned magenta, and Winter covered his eyes, dreading what was coming next. He could *feel* the energy building, knew with a hideous certainty what Tertia was going to do—

'*DISOBEDIENCE IS NOT ALLOWED!*' It came out as half-snarl and half-shriek, as Tertia prepared to launch what was probably intended to be her most spectacular telekinetic attack yet on Suuu. Before she could direct her energy, though, Sometimes uttered a loud neigh and reared high, hooves flailing the air. Tertia yelled in shock; reeling back she frantically switched her attention from Suuu to the horse. Sometimes froze in mid-rear, his forelegs locked and rigid. Then he started to rise from the floor. He rose very slowly; Tertia was grunting and gasping, her face growing redder still, and Suuu grinned again.

'Now you've upset him. He won't like you for that; he'll kick the daylights out of you if you release your hold on him. Which leaves Winter and me free to do whatever we like!'

Tertia's head snapped round as Suuu sauntered towards the Throne. She made an incoherent noise; Suuu stopped as if she'd smacked into a brick wall, and swayed on her feet.

'Uh-oh,' she said. 'She's stronger than I thought. Winter, quick – do something to annoy her!'

Winter believed he was beginning to understand. He

turned to the blank-faced crowd of celebs, who by now were all cowering in the farthest part of the room, and shouted, 'Go on, get out of here! All of you! *Scatter*!'

They stared at him like hypnotised sheep and did nothing. Then help came from a quite unexpected quarter.

'Ohh, this is *too* much!' It was Soho, elbowing through from the back of the gaggle. 'I shall sue my agent! I shall sue the Corporation! I shall sue *everyone*!'

She made a run for the door – and the entire flock of sheep surged after her. Tertia screamed and several cardboard pillars came tumbling down, but the chaos was too much for her. Trying to control everything at once, she lost control altogether. Sometimes dropped to the floor with a wallop and made his own protest known with some hefty kicks in every direction, and in the midst of the hullabaloo Winter felt his arm grabbed tightly.

'Run for it!' Suuu yelled in his ear.

He didn't stop to consider; he went with her. As they flung themselves towards the exit, Sometimes got a clear run at Tertia and charged straight for her. The last image Winter had was of Tertia racing for the stairs with the horse at her heels, then they were through the doors, through the babbling crowd (who, with no one to direct them, were all now milling aimlessly about) and sprinting down the nearest corridor.

'Suuu!' Winter called, panting. 'Suuu, wait! What have you—'

'No time to explain now!' Suuu shouted back. 'We've got to find Angel! *Angel! Where are you*?'

Still running, they both started to shout Angel's name,

Winter throwing Twinkle's in for good measure. They were near the door of New Players' Reception when, distantly, an answering call came back.

'Winter?'

'Yes, yes, it's Winter! Find Winter!'

A little gold-and-silver blur came hurtling round a corner, and Twinkle took a flying leap into Winter's arms. She licked his face ecstatically, and past the blur of her tongue Winter saw Angel appear.

'Oh, Tokyo, I was never so glad to see you!' She would have hugged him but Twinkle was in the way and Suuu was already tugging her towards a side turning.

'Quick!' Suuu urged. 'Outside!'

'In that storm?' Angel looked horrified, and tried to turn instead towards New Players' Reception. 'No way! The mirror-door—'

'We can't use it; Pye's doing something to it!' Suuu saw distrust on Angel's face and took a deep, gulping breath. 'Look, it's my truth time again, so I'm not going to screw anything up! But I don't know how long it'll last, and I've got to tell you what's going on before it changes, and unless we're out of this building Tertia might get control of us again. So come *on*!'

Angel hesitated a bare moment. Then: 'All right. I trust you!'

They ran towards the nearest outside door, and the full fury of the weather.

# TWELVE

With Suuu in the lead, the three of them made for the nearest path and went plunging down the perilous slope, skidding and sliding and grabbing at sodden bushes. The rain battered down on their heads, soaking them in secs, and small rivers rushed past their feet, hurtling downhill even faster than they were doing.

The storm was playing havoc with the castle's electronic systems. Behind them, lights flashed and danced in the windows, and all the gadgets in the bushes were going haywire, jumping up and crashing down and babbling nonsense at them. There were lamps on the path, but they crackled and sputtered and dipped as the power circuits fluctuated wildly. At one point Angel slipped and cannoned into one; it exploded with a *pop* and blue sparks fizzed in the downpour, to be answered by an even bluer flash of lightning. Thunder bellowed, and Angel scurried on.

How any of them got to the foot of the hill in one piece, Angel would never know, but just when she thought her legs or brain or both were going to give out on her, the path levelled out and they were on the harbour wall. She slid to a stop and doubled over, hands on knees, head hanging and water streaming from her hair as she gasped for breath.

'Where can we shelter?' Winter wanted to know.

Suuu shook herself like a dog. 'Shelter? Not a chance! We've got an appointment to keep, and that means getting to the mainland.'

Angel looked incredulously at Suuu, then at the harbour, which was like a scene out of a mad Vee programme. The noise of the sea sounded almost as loud as the noise of the thunder, and ceaseless into the bargain, and every few secs, or so it seemed to her, lightning lit up the scene in a spectacular glare, showing the rain driving like hosepipes and the swell heaving blackly against the quay wall. The tide was high and the causeway was probably under four metres of water.

She said, '*How?*'

'Boat, of course.' Suuu was quite unfazed. 'There's one here somewhere – probably leaks a bit, but it'll stay afloat long enough to get us there; it's only a short way. Come on. We'd better get moving, before Tertia comes after us.'

Angel argued. She argued while Winter and Suuu searched for and found the painted boat, with garish red-and-orange dinky seats in it, moored at the far end of the quay; she stood in the downpour and argued as they climbed in and Suuu fiddled with controls in the back end ('All right, the stern, then!' she shouted. 'But it won't matter what anyone calls it when it sinks!') and she was still arguing when Winter reached up to help her down the steps and into the craft. She would *not* get in that thing! She would rather face the mad castle and ten thousand Tertias than trust her life to a *boat*, on the *sea*, in *this* weather! And she didn't believe that anyone could seriously expect her to *try*!

She probably would have ranted on until she ran out of breath, but suddenly from somewhere nearby came a loud bleep. Startled, they all looked round for the source, and saw a metal pole with a box-like contraption on it. In the centre of the box was an eye-like lens, and beside the lens a red warning light was flashing on and off.

Suuu said, 'Uh-oh . . .' Then a sec later she added, 'Oh, *bother!*'

High above them an enormous glare had suddenly stabbed out into the night, and at the same moment a whining siren began to sound. A powerful beam was shining out from one of the castle's towers. It began to revolve, and though the movement was slow and jerky, it cut through the dark like a knife through froth.

'She's got an alarm system!' Suuu said. 'That searchlight's looking for us – we must have been picked up on some kind of sensor!'

The light dimmed, and for a sec or two actually went out. Then, with a huge flicker, it appeared again. Its angle had changed. Instead of sweeping far out to sea, it was directed down at the base of the island, and the questing beam was moving towards them.

'Angel,' said Suuu in a voice that wasn't going to take no for an answer, '*Move!*'

Angel moved. With Twinkle clinging to her neck and squawking, she scrabbled down the steps and jumped into the boat. Suuu fiddled in the stern, pulled something, thumped something else with a clenched fist, and a computer voice said, 'WELCOME ABOARD THE SAUCY SAL! WE'RE ALL GOING TO HAVE A

JOLLY SAIL, AND . . . *WUUUUURRGHHHH* . . .' The announcement collapsed in a damp hiccup, and a spluttering sound, together with a puff of smoke and a rank smell, came from a hidden depth.

'Hold tight!' said Suuu. 'Here we go!'

The boat's engine roared into life, Winter cast off, and they turned for the harbour mouth.

'Well, the engine sort of works, anyway,' Suuu shouted above the racket. 'So far, so good!' Another lightning flash lit up her grinning face, and Angel cringed, hunching down between two of the dinky little seats and gripping them with all her strength.

The swell met them and the boat began to pitch; instantly she felt sick and shut her eyes, not wanting to see the lightning or the heaving water. But not seeing them was worse, for her stomach decided to pitch in a different direction and rhythm to the boat's movement. Angel groaned, and Winter laughed.

'It isn't far to the mainland. You'll be all right! At least the rain's flattened the sea, so it's fairly calm.'

*If this is calm, what's it like when it's rough?* But Angel felt too ill to get the words out. Rain, lightning, thunder, waves, sickness, terror – she thought she was probably going to die. And right at this moment, it seemed like the best possible option.

She didn't die. Instead, she threw up over the side twice, then a third time while Winter and Suuu were hauling the boat up on to the beach. The world seemed slightly better after that, but her legs still felt like jelly as she trailed after them, away from the shore and towards the row of derelict buildings behind the broken sea wall. At the monorail terminus the tangle of wires and cables hung soggily down, and sparks hissed and spluttered around the gantries; one car had come loose and dangled from the rail by a single cable, swaying alarmingly. They skirted round it, and as Suuu hurried on, Angel demanded, 'Where are we going?'

'I told you, we've got an appointment. Now . . . the fourth door along, he said . . .'

'Who said?'

'You'll see! Come on – this is the place!'

They ducked under a low doorway with no door in it, into a huge, empty space. The storm-noise echoed hollowly in here, but it was sheer bliss to get out of the rain. Angel took a deep breath and started to squeeze water out of her hair and clothes.

Then she stopped dead as from the darkness a familiar voice said humorously, 'About time, too!'

'*Pye*!' Angel's eyes widened. An orange glow sprang to life, and there he was, smiling at them in the light of a small but powerful hand lamp.

'My dears!' Pye came forward and embraced them all. 'Well *done*!' Another thunderclap rattled the walls, and when the noise had died away sufficiently for anything else to be audible again, he continued.

'That was a good trick of yours, Winter, telling Suuu not to bring the devices back to me. She came straight to the workshop with them, of course. So I analysed the readings, and I found out a few useful things. Including the whereabouts of Tertia's other reality doors.'

'Other?' Angel and Winter said together.

'Indeed. She has several more dotted around. In fact, one of them is right here in this building.'

He raised the lamp higher, and from a far corner came an answering reflection.

'Tokyo!' Angel stared in astonishment at the familiar sculpture of mirrors and struts. Pye smiled. 'I was able to trace them all through Winter's readings, and now – with only two exceptions – I've shut them down.'

'What exceptions?' Winter asked.

'This one, of course, and the one in what she calls New Players' Reception.' Pye smiled. 'She probably doesn't even remember that this one exists; it was a prototype, I suspect, and it hasn't been used for some considerable time.' He walked towards the sculpture. 'Tertia's doors are slightly different to the ones I build. She's made some interesting modifications; including an automated setting and opening system, and no need for water jets. She's really very clever.'

'Dangerously clever!' Angel said with feeling.

'Ye-es. But not infallible. We have one useful weapon against her . . . or is it two?' He raised a questioning eyebrow in Suuu's direction.

Suuu nodded. 'Two. I did what you said: got her into a position where she had to try to control Sometimes and the rest of us at the same time.' She grinned. 'She couldn't do it.'

Winter's eyes lit. 'I thought so! She can only spread her energy so far – if she tries to concentrate on too many things at once, it all falls apart!'

139

'Exactly!' Pye said with satisfaction. 'I admit it was a gamble putting that to the test; but it appears to have paid off. Excellent! Now, I'm sorry that you had to meet me here, but I'm sure you understand that it would have been far too dangerous for me to appear in the castle. As it is, we've killed two birds with one stone, so to speak: by taking the boat, you've effectively marooned Tertia on the island until the tide goes out and the causeway can be crossed. That should give us the time we need to get ready.'

'You think she'll come after us?' Angel asked uneasily.

'She's probably lost interest in you by now. But we're going to change that. We're going to lure her out.'

'How?'

'With a game, of course. A brand new game that Tertia won't be able to resist.' Pye grinned conspiratorially. 'One that she *thinks* she can win.' He turned to a large bundle that lay near the mirror sculpture. 'I've brought some dry clothes for you all. You might think my choice is strange, but it's all part of my little scheme. Oh, and I've also brought something to eat, as I imagine Tertia's idea of food isn't particularly palatable.'

The words 'eat' and 'food' made Twinkle wriggle and raise her head. 'Hello, Pye,' she said forlornly. 'I got ever so wet. Did you bring anything for me?'

'Of course I did, my little friend; enough even for your appetite!'

Twinkle brightened. 'Goody!' Then she flattened her ears. 'I don't want to go on that boat thing again!'

'You shan't have to,' Pye promised. 'We'll get you dry, then feed you, and then we're going to play my brand new game.'

'Oooh,' said Twinkle. 'Will it be fun?'

Pye's hazel eye twinkled visibly. 'Yes,' he said. 'I think it will.'

The storm finally rumbled away into the northwest, leaving the night very quiet and still. The sea hardly made a murmur, and eventually the clouds cleared enough for the moon to show fitfully.

In the derelict building, the planning was complete; or as complete as it could ever be, considering the uncertainties involved. Pye had gone back to his workshop for the time being. He had been investigating Tertia's modifications to the mirror-door design, and planned to add a few more of his own devising. He had, however, left them with several new gizmos – and some very bizarre costumes.

As Pye had told Angel once before, Tertia was a peculiar mixture of wilful, unreasoning child and intelligent, cunning adult, and the two sides tended to clash. On the one hand, she was clever enough to have built and improved her own reality doorways; on the other, her behaviour was more often than not downright babyish. If she had been content to find a world of her own and play quietly in it, all might have been well. But her abilities allowed her to make her games too real. As far as she was concerned, people existed only to amuse and indulge her, and if anyone wanted to argue about it she used her telekinetic power to make sure they didn't argue twice. Whether she had used it to kidnap her cast of celebs, or whether she had simply bamboozled them into going along with her, probably no one would ever know, but it wasn't important. What mattered was putting a stop to her self-indulgent empire building, before someone got terminally hurt.

Pye's plan wouldn't have fooled a normal person for five secs; but Tertia was different. Rather like Twinkle, she was easily distracted by the pettiest of things – and distraction was the name of this new game. As soon as Tertia saw it begin, she would want to play. She would *demand* to play.

So they would all play it with her, until she just couldn't take any more.

The tide was going down by the time dawn began to creep over the horizon. The castle was in darkness; the searchlight had been switched off (or had gone wrong) some time ago, and since then things had been quiet.

The three of them had snatched some sleep, and had just woken up when the mirrors of the doorway flared and Pye returned. He was wearing a jacket and trousers in a stunningly loud clash of lime green and purple, and an enormous black hat with gold stars dangling and twinkling all round the brim.

'My costume!' he said breezily, then handed them a zoomviewer and told them to take a look at the castle.

'You should see signs of activity in a min or two,'

he said. 'Stage One is about to begin.'

They all took a turn with the zoomviewer's magnifying lens. At first there was nothing to look at – then suddenly, as Angel was looking, a puff of orange smoke burst above one of the castle towers, and a few secs later they heard a distant, muffled *bang*.

Angel looked suspiciously at Pye and said, 'What have you done?'

'Just a harmless little display, my dear Angel; to make sure that Tertia is wide awake when the real fun begins.' He grinned. 'I've also completed my work on the reality door in the castle, so we're all set.'

'It's woken them up, all right.' Winter had taken the zoomviewer and was peering through it. 'There are lights coming on, and people scurrying outside. I can't see Tertia, though.'

'She'll be there, depend on it.' Pye was rummaging in yet another of his seemingly endless supply of sacks, and brought out three metal cylinders, each pointed at one end and with a long string attached to it. 'Right. One for you . . .' handing the first to Winter, '. . . and one for you, and one for *you*.'

Angel looked dubiously at hers. 'Are you sure these are safe?'

'Safe as houses,' said Pye airily. 'But they do make rather a lot of noise, so be prepared for that. Now, have you all got your costumes? Good! Then I'll return to the castle and prepare for my little part in the proceedings.' He patted the crown of his hat. 'Don't you think I make an *excellent* Casting Director?'

He didn't wait for a reply, but stepped into the mirror sculpture and was gone.

Gazing down at herself in her costume, Angel could only come to the conclusion that she looked a complete snail. It was Pye's idea of the Top Corporate Exec look; shiny body-hugger that covered her from throat to knees, long boots with silly little wings on them, and half a tonne of garish jewellery dangling round her neck and arms. There was also an Incognito wraparound for her to put over her eyes; the sort of thing celebs wore when they wanted to be seen not being seen; but no way was she going to put that on until she absolutely had to.

Suuu and Winter were wearing their costumes, too, and Angel's only comfort was that they looked as ridiculous as she did. They both had tight breeches with huge flares above the knees, dazzlingly striped and spotted jackets with shoulders that stuck out half a mile, and hats with vast brims. They were Vee Directors. Even Twinkle had a coat with some fake gems stuck on, and a cat-sized Incognito. The little Therapet thought it was all wonderful, and had been preening and strutting ever since the things were put on her.

Angel glanced up again and saw Suuu watching her with a droll expression. 'Well,' Suuu said, 'aren't we the bees' elbows? Do you have circuses in your reality?'

'No,' said Angel.

'Oh. Never mind; it's not worth explaining. Here we go, then. Final check: has everybody got their props?'

Wordlessly Angel held up a fake and hugely oversized

soundpix recorder in one hand and an equally enormous furled banner, with a pole at either end, in the other. Winter grinned at her expression and picked up a large metal cone with a handle at one end. According to Pye, it was called a megaphone, and though he hadn't explained how, it apparently had the ability to make everyone in range listen, whether they wanted to or not. In the palm of his other hand he displayed a small, unobtrusive device.

'All here,' he said.

Suuu laughed, and tapped her hip, where another device was attached to her belt. 'All *righty*!' she said. She picked up a small case, and turned towards the door. 'Come on, folks – it's Show Time!'

It was full daylight now, and the beach was bathed in sunshine. Most of the causeway was appearing from under the water, with only a few metres still submerged. With Winter in the lead, the three of them marched down the slope and on to the sand. Twinkle started grumbling about the wetness and wanted to be carried, but Angel told her firmly that it was part of the game and she would just have to put up with it. Winter was taking readings from one of his devices, and at a point about midway between the sea wall and the tideline, he stopped.

'This is the place; the two mirror-doors are right in line.' With his foot, he drew a circle some two metres across in the sand. Then he unclipped a small sensor from the device he carried, and buried it at the circle's exact centre. Angel and Suuu watched as he took readings, made adjustments, took more readings. At last there was a faint *bleep* from the sensor, and the air above the circle shimmered briefly.

'Right.' Winter straightened. 'All ready. Let's set up the rest of our scene.'

He hurried off in the direction of the monorail terminus, and Angel and Suuu started to unfurl the banner. Putting it up was tricky; the wind kept catching it and once it almost blew away, but at last both poles were firmly planted in the sand. In huge black letters the banner proclaimed the words: 'SENIOR CONTRACTS EXEC' and underneath was an impressive but meaningless logo. Suuu flipped a catch on the case she had been carrying, and the case promptly unfolded itself and turned into a small desk with a drawer. From the drawer Suuu produced a pile of papers, which she put on the desk-top and weighted down with another pebble. The papers were printed with the words 'MEGA-CONTRACT' at the top and 'SIGN HERE' at the bottom; all that was needed, as Pye had said, to get a would-be celeb excited.

Winter came hurrying back. 'I've fixed the monorail,' he reported. 'You should be able to trigger the mechanisms with your belt device, Suuu.'

'Double-A,' said Suuu, catching Angel's expression. She squinted across the sea to the castle. 'Okay, then. I think it's fireworks time!'

Pye had assured them that the metal cylinders weren't dangerous, but all the same Angel's heart was thumping as she stood beside hers with the string in her hand. The three of them had spaced themselves out in a line along the beach, about twenty metres apart, and Winter was to give the signal to set the devices off. Twinkle (who had at last wheedled her way on to Angel's shoulder) wriggled and squeaked, 'Ooh! Isn't this exciting?'

'It'll be a bit *too* exciting if these things go wrong!' Angel told her. 'Shh! I'm trying to concentrate.'

Winter raised his arm, then dropped it, and all three of them pulled on the strings.

The triple bang of the launch was so loud that Twinkle jumped straight up in the air with shock, landing back on Angel's shoulder and digging all her claws in. Angel winced, catching a chaotic glimpse of the three cylinders hurtling skywards – then as one, they all exploded in a stunning shower of red, green and silver sparks. More deafening bangs echoed across the bay, and as the din receded Winter raised the megaphone to his mouth.

'OKAY, PEOPLE, LET'S GET MOVING! PLACES, PLEASE – BUSY-BUSY-*BUSY*!'

Pye timed it to perfection. As Winter's amplified voice bawled out, some twenty people came stumbling out of the derelict building behind them. For a few secs they milled around in confusion. That Casting Director back in the castle had told them about the new mega-Vee, but where were they supposed to *go*?

Then one of them saw the banner. And at the same moment Winter lifted the megaphone again.

'FLIT, PEOPLE, FLIT! SHOOTING'S ABOUT TO START, AND THE CONTRACTS DEPARTMENT IS RIGHT HERE! NO CONTRACT, NO PART – SO HURRY-HURRY-HURRY!'

A squeal went up, and there was a mass surge towards

the desk. Angel had taken up position behind it, and the people homed in on her like a swarm of bees.

'That must be the Senior Exec!'

'Coo-ee! Here I am!'

'I saw her first; get out of the way!'

'I've got a list of creds—'

'My agent says—'

'I've been sponsored by—'

Jostling and pushing, they crowded round Angel, all talking at once. Then a familiar figure elbowed her way to the front. Her Pretend Queen's clothes looked the worse for wear, and she didn't have a crown any more. But it took a lot to daunt Soho.

'*Divine* to meet you!' she gushed. 'Which – um – which Vidco would you be – um—'

'*The* biggest, sweetie, and *the* best,' said Angel airily. 'We're starting work on our new production right here and now. So, if you want a part, darling, you'd better zoom in for the audition!'

'Oh, abso-*mega*-lutely!' said Soho, then leaned to whisper confidentially, 'Of course, I really am far too much of a celeb to be in this little setup; I only agreed to help them out from kindness; you know how it scans . . . If you saw the list of my credits and my sponsors, you'd just *scream* with delight! How much do you pay? Where do I sign?'

Suuu, meanwhile, was scanning the castle through the zoomviewer, and suddenly she let out a piercing yell.

'It's worked!' She pointed excitedly towards the causeway. 'Here she comes – and the rest of them are coming with her!'

# THIRTEEN

Sometimes was coming down the path from the castle at quite a speed, and from the way Tertia was clinging to the saddle, it was obvious that she was no horsewoman. She had stepped her Queen image up a gear or three: she was dressed in dramatic black, with a ludicrously long crimson cloak flowing behind her (and getting tangled in Sometimes's hooves, much to his annoyance), and on her head was a golden crown twice the size of the one Soho had worn, with swathes of what looked like glittering Chiffonize attached to it and bouncing around her shoulders.

Behind came her royal retinue. Whether or not she had told them to come, it was impossible to judge, but they were scrambling and slithering in her wake. Queen's Soldiers tripped each other up with their wood and cardboard weapons, while Queen's Servants teetered and clutched each other and seemed mostly to be squabbling over who went first, last or in the middle. Angel was too busy handing out 'contracts' to take much in, but Winter ran to join Suuu.

Tertia and Sometimes reached the harbour, and suddenly Sometimes's head jerked stiffly up. 'She's using that energy of hers on him!' Suuu said angrily. 'His hooves aren't touching the ground properly. Cheek of it—'

Under Tertia's kinetic control the horse moved jerkily to the beginning of the causeway and started across. 'That might be a good thing,' Winter pointed out. 'She'll use up energy, and the more she uses, the better for us.' He smiled wickedly. 'It won't improve Sometimes's temper, either.'

Suuu brightened at the thought of Sometimes getting his own back on Tertia. 'Better get the scenario going,' she said. 'They'll be here in a min.'

She sprinted back to where Angel was still besieged by would-be megastars, and started to shout orders at everyone. Those who already had contracts began to run around at her direction; those who didn't have them yet urged Angel to give them something, *anything*, to sign, so that they wouldn't be left out. Winter watched through the zoom for a few secs longer. Tertia was close enough now for him to see her clearly; her mouth was open and she was yelling across the distance at them, but no one could hear her. Her face was beginning to turn puce with frustration. She was so furious that she temporarily released her hold on Sometimes, who suddenly began to object to the fact that part of the causeway was still under water. He didn't want to wade through it, and there was a sharp tussle during which several people got kicked and several more soaked before Tertia finally managed to reassert her kinetic control. She treated Sometimes to a vicious prod in the ribs, and forced him across the last few metres on to the sand. The entourage came sloshing and stumbling after, squeezing seawater from their clothes. They had seen the banner, and were starting to look very interested, but none of them dared push past. With a grim-faced Tertia on his back, Sometimes rose a few centimetres from the sand and began to drift towards the gathering.

'What's going on?' Tertia shouted. 'Who are you?'

Soho clasped her hands ingratiatingly as Tertia approached. 'She's an absolutely mega-Top Exec, Your Majesty,' she burbled. 'Her Vidco are going to make a new production, right here! Isn't that just *double-A*?'

Tertia stopped Sometimes and stared aggressively at Angel. 'I haven't given you Permission!' she snapped. 'You can't play games without my Permission; it's Not Allowed!'

Angel looked at her and gasped, 'Oh! Mag-NIF-icent!!'

Tertia was so surprised that she forgot about controlling Sometimes. All four of his legs came down with a jolt and he jumped sideways. Tertia bounced in the saddle and was thrown inelegantly on to his neck; her crown fell off and as she scrabbled to regain her balance, her mouth opened to yell in fury. But Angel beat her to it.

'Magnificent, *magnificent*! Such beauty, such brilliance! You have got to be the most *talented* celeb in all *history*, and if you don't take the starring role in my new game, I shall just *die* of misery!'

She ran towards Tertia, making what she hoped looked like Exec-style gestures. 'Please, darling, save my life and tell me you'll be my megastar! Fame and fortune, world tours; oh, you'll be *ultra*! You'll have thousands of celebs from thousands of realities *begging* to come here and be allowed to play!'

The entourage was staring at Angel now, and looking *extremely* interested. Someone whispered, 'She's a *really*

151

high-powered exec . . . Got to be!'

Tertia ignored them and glowered at Angel. 'We're already playing a game,' she said. 'It's called "Find The Traitors", and everybody's got to search very hard because failing to find them is Not Allowed. Whoever finds them gets a prize, and then we're going to play another game called "Executing The Traitors".' She tossed her head. 'It's a better game than *yours*.'

'Oh, it is, of course! But . . .' Angel held up a finger. 'There's one thing about our game that's utterly *delumptious*!' That was one of Soho's favourite words, she recalled; and one of her silliest. 'In our game, you'd be the *only* star. Here's the plot: you're a Queen, of course, and you have total power over a vast Queendom. But there's a wicked usurper who wants to take your Queendom away. You, of *course*, are so brilliant that you don't need anyone to help you. You triumph over your enemies *entirely* through your own talents, and then you Live Happily Ever After!'

Tertia began to waver; her conceit and selfishness were so great that she couldn't see through the sheer frothy nonsense of what she was being offered. But suddenly her frown came back. 'No!' she said pettishly. 'We only play *my* games here!'

'But the Wicked Usurper scenario *is* your game,' Angel put on a convincing look of surprise. 'I'm sure you just said so.' She turned to the others. 'Didn't the Queen just say it's her game?'

There were cries of, 'Oh, yes!' 'Absolutely!' 'No doubt of it!'

'And your idea of combining both scenarios – Usurpers and Traitors – is truly *mega*!'

'I didn't—'

'Wait, wait; I can see it!' Angel rushed on before Tertia could get another word in. 'As well as saving your Queendom, you find the traitors and earn the eternal gratitude and admiration of your subjects! Where are my Directors?' She raised her voice to its full pitch. 'DIRECTORS! Scenario change – the Queen's got a new idea, and it's completely over the stars!'

Suuu and Winter stopped Directing and came running to join them. Suuu took a sweeping look at the whole scene and shouted, 'Perfect, perrr-FECT! Okay, let's get moving, busy-busy-busy; no slackers and everybody on their toes!' while Winter snatched the fake soundpix from Angel and pretended to peer through it as he pranced towards Tertia. 'Oh, wow!' he enthused. 'Just wait till I get lighting on this fabulous Queen! The costume, the hair, the face, the unbelievable *star quality*!'

Tertia nearly fell off Sometimes in her efforts to watch both Suuu and Winter as they ran in circles around her, babbling praise. Again her control lapsed; Sometimes took his chance, and this time he made sure of it. He gave a terrific buck that sent Tertia flying straight over his head, to land with an undignified thump on the sand. Luckily for all those who couldn't resist laughing, her scream of fury drowned out all other noises, and Sometimes stood looking pleased with himself.

Belatedly, soldiers ran to help Tertia to her feet. She was so angry that for a few secs she couldn't call up anything but wordless splutterings; then just as it looked as if she really would cause some serious damage, Winter raised the megaphone.

'ANNOUNCEMENT!' The sheer volume of the noise stopped everyone in their tracks. Even Winter was jolted, but he quickly recovered. 'THE HORSE IS A BAD HORSE, AND IS NOT WORTHY OF OUR WONDERFUL QUEEN!' he continued. 'ALL BOW TO OUR WONDERFUL QUEEN!'

Celebs obeyed directors as a matter of course. They all bowed . . . and a little of the rage ebbed from Tertia's eyes.

Winter bawled out: 'FROM NOW ON, THE HORSE IS NOT ALLOWED! THE QUEEN WILL HAVE SOMETHING BETTER! SHE WILL HAVE . . . THE ROYAL BARGE!'

He pointed at the boat, then dropped the megaphone and turned to Tertia with a helpless look. 'Only problem is, how to move it. The engine doesn't work any more.'

'I can move it!' Tertia said scornfully. 'Watch me!'

She swung round, showing a sand-covered back, and concentrated. The beached boat, some twenty metres away, rocked. Then it started to slide along the sand towards them. It moved very slowly and it obviously took a lot of Tertia's energy to keep it going, but she was so intent on showing off that she didn't think about conserving her strength. Behind her back, Angel grinned . . .

'There!' The boat stopped moving and Tertia turned triumphantly, panting. 'I'm the Queen. I can do anything I want to!' She hesitated, then glared at Angel. 'I *might* let you play my game of Saving the Queendom. But you'll have to play it the way *I* say!'

'Absolutely!' Angel gushed, and Winter lifted the megaphone again. 'THE QUEEN DECREES THAT WE'RE ALL GOING TO PLAY "SAVING THE QUEENDOM"! GET YOUR CONTRACTS – THE SCENARIO STARTS *NOW!*'

Uttering cries and whoops, all the people who had followed Tertia over the causeway rushed for the Contracts desk. They might have been scared of Tertia, but they were more scared of missing out on a chance of stardom. As they came piling in, Angel grabbed one 'contract,' shoved the rest at the first arrival, and dodged round the desk as Suuu hurried past, chivvying a batch of celebs into their places.

'Time to step things up!' Angel hissed. 'Remember what Pye said.'

An odd frown appeared on Suuu's face. 'No, I . . .' She paused, and the frown abruptly cleared. 'Yes. Make a lot of things happen at once, that was it.' She looked relieved. 'Right!'

She sprinted off; Winter saw her and nodded to Angel, then hefted the megaphone once more. 'SCENE ONE, TAKE ONE! THE QUEEN IS BESIEGED BY TRAITORS, AND HER LOYAL SUBJECTS TRY TO HELP HER! HALF OF YOU ARE TRAITORS, THE OTHER HALF ARE SUBJECTS! FIGHT FOR YOUR QUEEN – I WANT ACTION, I WANT DRAMA, I WANT *PASSION!*'

About fifteen act-fights instantly broke out on the

beach, peppered with groans and cries and theatrical caperings. Tertia hadn't expected that, and she shouted, 'Stop it! I didn't say Go! Nobody does anything until I say Go!'

They were all acting too enthusiastically to take any notice of her. Furious, Tertia ran towards the nearest fighting group. She was heading for the circle Winter had drawn in the sand; it was trampled now but still just visible, and Angel held her breath, hope leaping. But just before she reached the circle Tertia stopped. Her face turned ugly, and she stiffened, preparing to launch a kinetic attack.

Angel yelled a warning to Suuu. Suuu saw, and her hand went to her belt—

There was a groan, a rattle and an electronic whine from the direction of the monorail terminus, and one of the cars began to move. Tertia's jaw dropped. 'That's Not Allowed!' she yelped. 'Those are *mine*, nobody touches them without permission! I haven't given permission! *Stop!*'

Angel felt the energy charge raise hairs on her neck as Tertia focused her power. The car started to rock wildly; then Tertia made a sharp gesture, and it suddenly accelerated and hurtled towards the end of the rail. It hit the rusty barrier, there was a dire crunching sound as the barrier crumbled, and the car overshot the rail and catapulted towards the beach.

This time the screams were genuine as people in the car's path scattered. It soared over their heads, nose-dived into the sand with a dull thud, and fell apart.

Tertia shrieked: '*Everyone STOP!*'

Everyone did stop, and the silence was acute as they all

stood rigid, watching her. Tertia swayed on her feet, steadied herself, and brushed her hands together. There was murder in her eyes as she scanned the fearful faces around her, and when she spoke again her voice was ominously quiet.

'I want,' she said, 'that Contracts person. Right *now*.'

Suuu and Winter, who were near to each other, exchanged uneasy looks and tried to see where Angel was. They couldn't find her. Tertia waited, tapping one foot impatiently . . . then a single voice spoke up.

'Oh, *here* she is! Coo-ee, everyone! I've found her!'

A waving hand appeared above the crowd, and Soho pushed her way to the front. She had hold of Angel's arm; Angel was arguing and trying to pull away, but other people decided that Soho wasn't going to take all the credit and grabbed Angel too, towing her helplessly along.

Tertia pointed at the sand a metre in front of her and snarled: '*Here*!'

They stood Angel on the appointed spot and all jostled for the best position. Soho started to gush, 'I was really the one who found her, so if it means a better role, I honestly think I should—'

'Shut up,' said Tertia. She studied Angel for what seemed a very long time. Then: 'I've seen you before.'

'No,' said Angel desperately. 'You haven't, definitely not!'

'I *have*,' Tertia repeated. 'You had an animal on your shoulder just now. I've seen that before, too; a very stupid and greedy animal.'

Twinkle had, in fact, fallen off Angel's shoulder in the mêlée and was now among the shuffling feet on the sand.

She was ruffled and cross, and Tertia's insult was the last straw. Shoving her head between a pair of ankles, she glared up at Tertia and announced, '*Not* stupid! Pooey!'

Tertia looked down at her. Then she looked at Angel again. Then she made a gesture, and Angel's Incognito went spinning away as if an invisible hand had hurled it, revealing her face.

Recognition dawned and Tertia said: 'I know who you are – you're the Traitor!' Up came her hand once more, and there was an approving gasp from the crowd as Angel rose into the air.

'The Traitor, oh yes, the Traitor!' 'What a brilliant scenario!' 'What happens now?' 'This is so *exciting*!'

'You stole my Magic Cat!' Tertia snarled. '*And* you spoiled my game. That's *Not Allowed*!'

Winter, five metres away, clutched Suuu's arm ferociously. 'We've got to do something!'

Suuu didn't answer; in fact she didn't even seem to hear him. Her face had screwed itself into an extraordinary expression . . .

'*Suuu*!' He elbowed her, hard. 'Tertia's going to do something terrible – we've got to get her into that circle, *fast*!'

Suuu snapped out of her trance and blinked. 'Er – sure. Look, I . . .' Again she hesitated, then shook her head as if to clear it. 'Quick – give me the megaphone thing! I'll distract her, get her to move into position, and you be ready to trigger the doorways at my signal!'

Winter nodded curtly. 'Just make sure Angel isn't in range when I do it!'

'No way!' Grabbing the megaphone, Suuu ran forward. 'NEW SCENARIO!' she bawled. 'PLACES, EVERYBODY, FOR THE TRAITOR SCENE!'

Tertia whirled, her concentration interrupted, and Angel jerked in the air like a puppet on strings.

'COME ON, FOLKS!' roared Suuu through the megaphone. 'GOOD EVENING—' she jolted, looking aghast. 'No, no, *no*! Not now, of *all* times! Oh, *stop* it—'

Winter's eyes widened as he realised what was happening. Suuu's truth time was ending. She had felt the change coming on in the last few mins; she was fighting it, but it was a losing battle.

'WE'RE DEFINITELY NOT HERE TO FOOL ANYONE, AND – oh, *damn*!'

'Keep control!' Winter shouted. 'Hold it back!'

'I *can't*! I mean, I can! Who are you, anyway? *Owww* – AND PYE ISN'T PLANNING TO LURE TERTIA INTO A TRAP—'

Tertia screeched, '*What did you say*?' She took a menacing step towards Suuu, who was shaking like the jelly that was another of Twinkle's favourite foods. '*Did you say PYE*?'

'No!' Suuu wailed. 'I mean, yes!' She dropped the megaphone, struggling to stop the change from overwhelming her. But she might as well have tried to stop the tide from going out. 'I always tell the truth!' she cried. 'Pye isn't really hiding in the castle! And you're not really a dangerous menace who ought to be put in a cage! Oh, Winter, *help*!'

Winter had no chance to help, for before he could

move a centi, Tertia tensed like an enraged animal. She started to scream; the scream rose to an ear-splitting pitch and the air around her blurred.

'*NOW . . . I . . . AM . . . CROSS . . .*' People went staggering backwards as though a hurricane had hit them, as Tertia gathered her strength for a single, devastating energy bolt. She flung both arms skywards; the air crackled; Angel shrieked as she was spun around like a child's toy—

And with a squall of fury, a small shape hurled itself at Tertia.

'*Angel's my friend! You leave her alone!*' Twinkle pounced on Tertia's nearest foot, and sank her teeth into it. Tertia yelled; her control snapped, and Angel crashed to the sand.

'Twinkle, get away from her!' Without any thought for her own safety Angel scrambled to her feet and charged into the fray. Twinkle was attached to Tertia's foot, growling furiously as Tertia hopped and danced in an effort to shake her off. Angel cannoned into her; all three of them reeled sideways—

And the air around them shimmered.

Angel made a lunge at Twinkle and snatched her away from Tertia. She shoved the little Therapet out of reach; then moved to dive after her. Suuu saw Winter's hand go to the trigger device, and she also saw the terrible mistake he was about to make. With a huge effort she dragged her mind under control, and mustered a last shred of truth.

'Winter! DON'T DO IT!'

Winter heard her, and logic said: *she's lying*. He hit the trigger.

Tertia and Angel vanished.

# FOURTEEN

Tertia's yell as the world turned inside-out seemed to come from sixteen different directions at once. Angel felt herself falling, spinning, righting herself again, then suddenly the scene cleared.

And she found herself amid a blaze of light, face to face with four Tertias.

The Tertias stared back at her, then in perfect unison each one raised a hand, and Angel realised that she was looking at the real Tertia and three mirror reflections. She couldn't see the mirrors, and there was no sign of her own reflected image, but Tertia, too, was obviously confused, for she lowered her hand again and said through clenched teeth, 'Stop this at once! It's Not Allowed!'

She glared at a point to Angel's right as she said it, then abruptly her head flicked left. 'And you! There's only supposed to be one of you! *Stop it!*'

A new light flickered and a doorway appeared. Beyond it Angel glimpsed the outlines of Tertia's Throne Chamber; then the scene wavered and changed, becoming instead a corner of the castle gardens. With an impact that was almost physical, Angel knew what had happened. Pye had set up a link between the two mirror doorways – one in the castle and the other in the derelict building on the mainland – so that, when a signal was triggered, anyone in direct line between them would be snatched out of Tertia's play-world and into another dimension. The dimension wasn't real; it was to be used as a kind of halfway station, to hold Tertia in check until Pye had arranged matters to ensure that she could do no more harm.

But Angel, too, had been caught in the trap. In a few mins Pye would close this halfway station – and if she didn't find the way out, she would be locked together with Tertia, just the two of them, forever.

Panic hit her like a deluge of icy water and she spun round, only to find herself faced with four more flickering, unreal doorways.

'Pye!' she shouted. 'It's me, it's Angel! I'm caught in here! *Pye!*'

'No!' Tertia screamed. 'There's no such person as Pye! There isn't allowed to be! I'm the Queen, and everybody's got to do what I say!' She raised her hand again: six more mirror-Tertias sprang to life out of the gloom, and Angel felt the air crackle. Tertia flung her kinetic bolt – and the energy ricocheted between the reflections in a chaotic backwash that surged over Tertia and sent her spinning crazily around.

Angel heard Tertia's shriek, but didn't wait to see what would happen next. There were doorways all around her, images jumping and dancing in a mad whirl – she saw one that seemed to have a corridor beyond, and she flung herself towards it. The scene around her warped, shifted, twisted into a new perspective, and, as fast and as frantically as she had ever done in her life, Angel ran.

★   ★   ★

'*No!*' Winter threw himself to his knees at the spot where Angel and Tertia had vanished. He scrabbled for the sensor buried in the sand, shook it, punched it, hit the trigger of the device in his hand. But it had no more effect than Twinkle, who was running round in circles and crying Angel's name.

A shadow fell across Winter and he looked up, breathing harshly, to see Suuu standing beside him.

'It's useful,' Suuu said dismally. 'She's here.'

There was a huge constriction in Winter's chest and his voice was savage. 'You told me not to do it!'

'I was lying. It wasn't the last moment before I changed. Who are you, anyway?'

Through the daze of his fury and fear Winter remembered Suuu's bizarre upside-down way of talking when she was in lies mode, and understood what she was telling him. This wasn't her fault. It was his. And he only had a few mins to put right the terrible mistake he had made.

'Suuu—'

'Never heard of her.'

*Oh, Tokyo . . .* But he had to try. 'Suuu, when the device triggered, it was supposed to trap Tertia in a new dimension between the mirror doorways. But Angel's trapped with her!'

'That's all right, then,' said Suuu.

Winter could have screamed. '*Listen* to me! In a few more mins, Pye's going to – I mean, Pye *isn't* going to shut down the only exit from that dimension! We've got to – to – to *fail* to get to him and warn him! Do you understand?'

Suuu looked up at the sky and whistled a little tune. Wildly, Winter looked around for Sometimes, thinking to jump on his back and ride for the causeway. But Sometimes had wandered off, and even if he could catch him there simply wasn't *time* for him to get to the castle before the mins ran out . . .

Something nudged his ankle and a little voice said, 'Winter . . .'

It was Twinkle, looking up at him with piteously bewildered eyes. 'Where's Angel gone?' she pleaded.

Winter's eyes lit. Twinkle might be small, but she was no ordinary cat. Thanks to Pye's tinkering, she had a turn of speed, if she needed it, that would leave most animals standing . . .

'Twinkle!' He dropped to a crouch. 'You can help Angel!'

'Goody!' Twinkle visibly brightened. 'How?'

'Pye's in the castle, over there on the island.' Winter pointed. 'Run to him as fast as you can, and tell him . . .' *Don't make it too complicated for Twinkle to remember . . .* 'Tell him that Angel's still with the Queen person.'

Twinkle growled. 'Don't like her!'

'I know. So we've got to save Angel from her, and we've got to do it quickly! Run to Pye, Twinkle! Give him the message!'

Twinkle blinked. For a moment or two she looked uncertain. Then: 'Yes! Find Pye! Tell Pye!'

Her hind paws kicked up a flurry of sand as she took off towards the causeway. Winter looked for the zoomviewer, but it was lost somewhere. He'd just have to trust that Twinkle made it in time, that she didn't get distracted by something along the way . . .

An elbow nudged him. Suuu had sauntered back, and said conversationally. 'All those people who aren't celebs, and aren't here anyway, are ignoring us.'

Winter swung round. The gaggle of would-be actors had gathered at the edge of the circle. Some stared with curious interest at the trampled sand; most, though, stared at Winter, their expressions hopeful.

Someone said: 'Um . . . is that the end of the scene? What happens next?'

'Maybe it's Lunch,' another suggested brightly. 'Is it?'

'Meal breaks *are* in the contract. I'm sure they are . . .'

Winter made a gargling noise and rushed past, barging them out of the way. They said things like, 'Well, *really*!' and 'The last Director I worked for didn't behave like this!' But Winter was ignoring them, and running towards the derelict building. For a few secs they all watched him go. Then, because there seemed to be nothing better to do, they started to trail slowly after him.

Angel ran – and Tertia was behind her.

Where Tertia had got the sword from Angel didn't know, and didn't want to know. She wasn't even sure that it was real, though the clang it made when Tertia had swung it at her, missed and hit the wall had sounded alarmingly solid.

Another doorway loomed to her left. For one heart-stoppingly wonderful moment it looked like the entrance to New Players' Reception, where the mirror sculpture was, but even as Angel rushed through it, its appearance changed and it became yet one more unending corridor. Struggling with crushing disappointment, Angel paused just long enough to drag some breath into her lungs, then ran on.

She was tiring. She wouldn't be able to keep running for much longer, and was only thankful that Tertia's long dress and ludicrous trailing cloak were hampering her and slowing her down. Tertia hadn't forgotten that Angel was a Traitor, and now she had also got the idea in her head that if she could catch and execute the Traitor, the world would magically return to normal. Tertia wasn't going to give up that idea. And she wasn't going to give up the pursuit.

Angel didn't dare shout for Pye any more. Firstly, she didn't believe that she could be heard outside of this limbo; secondly, shouting took the breath she sorely needed for running – and thirdly, the sound of Pye's name sent Tertia into a towering rage that brought a new energy surge hurtling in Angel's direction. The surges were weaker than they had been, but they could still do damage, as Angel had discovered when a section of ceiling above her head caved in and she only just got clear in time. That one had backfired on Tertia, for she had had to clamber over the resulting rubble. But next time, Angel might not be so lucky.

And time was running faster than she ever could. There *was* a way out, she *knew* there was. But this half-dimension held so many illusions, confusions, twists and turns that finding the one thread of reality was next to impossible.

From somewhere behind her came a high-pitched,

ululating cry. It was Tertia's latest noise, designed to frighten and impress the Traitor, and it sounded far too close for comfort.

Angel raced on.

Twinkle was pleased with herself. She hadn't forgotten the message she was to give to Pye, and she had only stopped to eat one mouthful of the lovely strawberries that grew alongside the path up to the castle. Pye was close by; she could feel his presence ahead of her, and she put on a last, galloping spurt as the door of New Players' Reception appeared ahead.

There was a lot of light flickering in the room, and at first Twinkle couldn't see Pye at all. Then the circuits of her eyes adjusted themselves, and there he was, bent over the mirror-thing and looking very busy.

Twinkle didn't really trust the mirror-things; they had led, in her opinion, to too much trouble. But she made herself move close to it, and nugded Pye's leg with her nose.

Pye jumped, then looked down. 'Twinkle! Whatever are you doing here?'

'Got a message,' said Twinkle self-importantly. 'From Angel.' She frowned. 'No . . . from *Winter*.' Her eyes crossed for a sec or two as she thought very hard. 'Winter says, Angel's still with the Queen person.'

Pye's own eyes all but popped out of his skull. 'Hell's bells! Twinkle, are you *sure* that's what Winter said?'

'Ever so sure.' Twinkle blinked hopefully. 'Have you got anything to eat?'

'*Eat*? Ye gods and small fishes, this is no time to think of food!' Pye whirled round, hands reaching towards an array of gadgets that he had set up on a table. One gadget was a timepiece. It was steadily counting down towards zero, and when Pye saw how many mins were left, he was horrified.

'Twinkle!' He snatched up a gizmo from the table. 'You can sense Angel, can't you? You can sniff her out?'

Twinkle nodded. 'I'm ever so good at that. It's fun!'

'Then we're going to have some fun now. Come on – there's no time to lose!'

He hoicked Twinkle up, tucked her under his arm and strode to the mirror sculpture. The gadget in his hand started to bleep; Pye pressed his thumb to a sensor pad and the bleeps resolved into a whine that went up and down the scale, until abruptly it settled on a single, steady note.

'That's it!' *I hope*, Pye added to himself, grimly. 'Hold tight, Twinkle – we're going after Angel!'

The mirrors lit up, and a sec later New Players' Reception was empty.

'AN-GEL!' Pye's voice echoed and re-echoed through the half-real corridors and rooms. 'AN-GEL! Twinkle, stop wriggling!'

'Can't!' said Twinkle. 'Tickles!' She made a gurgling sound that was her version of a giggle.

'Well, get down here, then, and start trying to find out where Angel is. But for goodness' sake don't run off and get lost!'

He set the little cat down on the floor. Twinkle shook herself, then started to sniff around. Her ears swivelled forward, then sideways in opposite directions, then backwards. Suddenly they stopped and pricked up.

'That way!' she announced.

Praying she was right, Pye headed for a doorway that had just appeared in what, before, had been a blank wall. Multi-reflections of Twinkle appeared momentarily, then they were hurrying along a passage that curved round in a long spiral.

'AN-GEL!'

'Angel, Angel! Yoo-hoo! Where are you? Ooh, this is a good game!'

There was no point, Pye told himself, in trying to explain to Twinkle that this was most certainly not a game, and he cursed himself. He had set the trap to close, ultimately and finally, at a prearranged time, and once the countdown had begun, even he could not stop it. There had been a reason for that, but Pye had assumed nothing would go wrong. It had gone wrong. Well, more fool him! Now, if Twinkle failed in her task, Tertia would have three companions to share her prison, and there would be nothing any of them could do about it.

He was opening his mouth to call Angel's name again when Twinkle's tail stood up like a flagpole and she bounced on the spot on all four paws.

'She's here, she's here!' she squeaked. 'Angel!'

She streaked ahead of Pye – and met Angel coming round the next curve in the passage. Angel's eyes widened with joy, then disbelief, then—'

'Oh, Pye, Pye!' She flung herself at him and gave him a breathtaking hug. 'I thought I'd never find you; I thought I'd never get out; and Tertia—'

'No time for talking, dear girl!' Pye untangled himself from her embrace. 'We've got just about two mins to make our escape.' Rapidly, he tapped out a pattern on the device he carried. The whining note started to swoop and dip again, and Pye muttered: 'Two left . . . then four right . . . then straight ahead, and – *yes*! Come on!'

He pointed the gizmo at the wall. Light flashed, and a doorway appeared. Beyond it was what looked like the tower room with the lightning conductor, where Angel had been imprisoned. Angel shrank back but Pye said, 'It's all right, it's perfectly safe!' and pushed her through. In the room, he pointed the gizmo again, and another door showed the castle garden. Four more times Pye conjured new doorways, then suddenly they were in a room where there were no more doorways, and no more reflections.

Angel stopped and stared around. The room *looked* like Tertia's Throne Chamber, but . . . there were differences. For one thing, there had been no windows in here before. For another, there was no staircase, and no Throne. And it all looked very solid; real stone rather than tacky wood and cardboard . . .

Confused, she turned to Pye. 'Where are we?'

Pye was thumbing the gizmo again. 'If I'm right – and I think I am – then this is our stepping off point. There's just one thing I need to check . . .'

He hurried to the nearest window, and Angel followed.

What she saw when she looked out made her start with surprise.

They were in the castle, and it was on an island. But the mainland was much further away, with no sign of buildings there, only empty sand dunes. And below them, where the sea shimmered, there was no harbour, no boat, and no causeway.

A dozen questions tumbled through Angel's mind, but she had no chance to ask them as Pye hurried back to the middle of the room. 'Small gods be praised!' He sounded hugely relieved. 'Now all we have to do is create a direct exit . . .'

More thumbing; again the whining noise swooped, hunted, settled; this time to a shrill, urgent note. Pye pointed the gizmo, and where the Throne should have stood, something else began to appear. At first it was distorted and unrecognisable, like something seen through a fish-eye lens. But after a few secs the clashing realities began to blend and squeeze themselves into shape, and the object resolved into a mirror sculpture, with the contours of New Players' Reception dimly visible beyond.

'Quickly!' Pye urged. 'By my calculation we've got less than a min!'

He chivvied Angel and Twinkle towards the sculpture – then suddenly, from behind them, there came a spectacular crashing and banging noise, accompanied by a yodelling yell.

Twinkle's fur stood on end and she snarled as Tertia came barrelling through the door. Tertia's eyes were alight with the zeal of battle; she was clutching the sword in both hands and swinging it around her head. The crashing and banging was the sound of the sword hitting the door frame, from which chunks of masonry were falling as if steel-hard teeth had taken bites out of it.

Tertia saw Pye, and skidded to a halt. Her shoulders hunched and her head went down. 'So it *is* you . . .' she growled.

'Good day to you, Tertia.' Pye appeared calm, but Angel looked at his eyes and knew he was anything but.

'*You*,' snarled Tertia, 'are *Not Allowed* . . .'

She took a step forward, kicking her trailing cloak aside. Then she lowered the sword until it pointed directly at Pye. She swung it, very fast; Angel heard the *whop* of displaced air. And her other hand began to rise, the fingers curling and clenching.

Angel clutched at Pye's arm. 'Let's make a run for the mirror-door!'

'No!' Pye shook his head quickly. 'It's too great a risk. If she throws a charge and hits the door before it closes, the heavens alone know what could become of us. Start to shuffle back. But very, very slowly . . .'

His foot slid a few centis and Angel followed suit. Twinkle was still growling and didn't move; Angel hissed, trying to get her attention, but Twinkle took no notice.

Tertia took another step. She was breathing very deeply and very steadily; a bad sign, Angel thought, for it meant she was really concentrating on building up her kinetic control. If she had enough strength left to snare them both, Angel imagined what would happen to them: dangling helpless under her power, while she played a new game with them and the sword . . .

A small whimper came from her throat, and Tertia smiled with huge pleasure. Pye's foot slid again. The mirror sculpture was no more than a metre behind them. But then Tertia laughed.

'I know what you're doing,' she said. 'But you won't get through. I'll stop you, because I'm the Queen.' She flexed her fingers again. 'You're scared of me, aren't you? Good. It's *fun* when people are scared of me. And you're going to be even more scared soon, because I've got my Magic Power, and my Magic Sword . . . oh yes – and my Magic Cat again.' She looked at Twinkle. 'Come here, Magic Cat.'

Twinkle's ears flattened. 'Shan't!'

Tertia's smile vanished and Angel hissed, 'Twinkle, no! Don't make her cross!'

'Don't,' Tertia agreed warningly. 'Because you know what happens when I get *cross*. You didn't like it last time. So come here, *now*.'

Twinkle glared rebelliously at her and said, 'Shan't-won't-can't-make-me! *Pooey*!'

Angel shut her eyes, appalled, and expecting the worst. But Pye knew Tertia better, and a spark of eager hope leaped in him. 'Angel!' he mouthed, and grasped tight hold of her hand. 'Be ready . . .'

Tertia leaned over Twinkle, who was bristling like a bottlebrush now. 'What did you say to me . . .?' she demanded menacingly.

'Said POOEY!' Twinkle retorted. 'Say it again! POOEY, POOEY POOEY!'

'*How dare you talk to the Queen like that!*' Tertia yelled furiously. Her hand shot out towards the cat – and Pye shouted, '*Now!*'

Yanking Angel with him, he dived for the mirror sculpture.

There was another yell, a clatter, an indignant catty yowl. Angel cried, 'Twinkle! Pye, don't leave her—' then everything turned on its head as two realities collided. Images of the Throne Chamber and New Players' Reception clashed and tangled with each other, and there were four Pyes and sixteen Tertias all dancing and jiggling in flaring mirrors, and someone was screaming, and the ceiling was caving in again, and sword-blades whirled and slashed and—

'*Nooo! How dare you! It's Not—*'

'*POOEY!!*' A small furry blur rocketed out of the sculpture and skidded into hiding . . .

Under Pye's table in New Players' Reception.

Angel clutched at the nearest solid surface to stop herself from keeling over. Dizzily her brain registered Pye at the sculpture, fingers flying on his control device; then from inside the sculpture came a rumble . . .

'Out!' Pye bawled. '*Fast!*'

He hauled Twinkle bodily from under the table and charged through the open door on Angel's heels. The door slammed with a wallop that shook the flimsy walls – then from inside New Players' Reception came an almighty BANG. The force of it threw them all to the floor, and as the echoes faded Angel raised her head.

'What . . . was . . . it?'

Pye picked himself up, rubbing bruises and coughing in the clouds of dust that eddied everywhere. 'That, my dear Angel, was the last we will ever see of Tertia's reality doorways. And the last we will ever see of Tertia.'

A small, muffled voice said, '*Goody*!' and Twinkle spat out the torn piece of black fabric she had been grasping between her teeth. 'Ptoo! Nasty stuff! Don't want to eat that!'

'That looks like—' Angel began.

'A piece of Tertia's dress?' Pye grinned at her. 'Quite. She really should have known better than to wear something so long. I thought from the start that it was likely to trip her up. So, it seems, did Twinkle.' He bent down and patted the little cat. 'Well *done*, Twinkle. You were very clever.'

Twinkle preened. She hadn't actually *planned* to dive between Tertia's feet and take a bite out of her dress, but Tertia had made her *cross*, so she'd done it, and then the material had got caught up in her teeth, and . . . well, she needn't bother explaining all that to Angel and Pye, need she?

Angel moved stiffly towards the nearest window, needing air. 'Has she really gone?' she asked.

'Oh, yes.' Pye assured her.

'Where . . . I mean, she isn't . . .'

'Dead? No, no. She's alive and well. But from now on she'll be living in a new reality of her very own.' Pye smiled. 'A few dimensional adjustments . . . but I won't bore you with the technicalities. You saw her new world for yourself. It's very like this one, but with just a few *teeny* differences. Such as, no materials for her to build a new mirror doorway. And no means – unless she chooses to swim the distance, which I rather doubt – of leaving the castle and the island.'

'Won't she starve to death?' Whatever her opinion of Tertia, Angel didn't like that thought at all. But Pye shook his head.

'I'll make sure she survives. An occasional visit through a temporary doorway on the mainland; an automated boat to deliver supplies and some Vee games to keep her entertained . . . I really think she'll be happier than she's ever been. But no one else will be forced to share her happiness.' He looked out of the window. 'Ah. I suspect that our little explosion was noticed on the beach. We seem to have a deputation approaching.'

Angel looked. A crowd of people were coming across the causeway. Without a zoomviewer it was impossible to pick out much detail, but Sometimes was there, with Suuu (presumably) riding him. And leading them all was a figure whom, even at this distance, she recognised at once. After all, no one could ever mistake Winter's white hair . . .

She smiled, then began to grin, despite the fact that she was feeling utterly exhausted. 'Shall we go and meet them?' she asked.

'Yes!' said Twinkle enthusiastically. 'And then we can all have some *food*!'

# CLEARING UP . . .

'It's been the most *marvellous* experience!' Soho clasped her hands together and simpered at Pye. 'Quite over the *stars*! I'll have so many anecdotes to tell my friends, and when my sponsors find out who I was really working for . . . well!'

Pye smiled back. 'Not too many Traumatic Episodes, I hope?'

'Pff!' Soho waved a hand airily. 'What real celeb doesn't go through trauma in pursuit of true art?' She looked at Angel and Winter, who were hovering in the background. 'Mega to have shared our talents, darlings. And you . . .' to Angel. 'You *are* a little like the daughter I used to have, though of course she was *far* less sophisticated; a trial to me, in fact; she never could understand or appreciate the important things of life . . .' She sighed. 'Ah, well. Poor Angel: such a pity she ran away . . . But I expect she's living happily in some frightful ethnic Zone and doing terribly serious things like Philosophising and Preparing Her Own Food. That's Angel all over.'

Angel looked away, tearfully, and Pye said, 'Well, goodbye, Soho. And thank you *so* much for your contribution to our little – um – production.'

'Any time, any time! You have my agent's vid? Wonderful! Must flit, then – busy-busy-busy. That's the

Vee door, yes? Goodbye, sweeties!'

The mirrors flared, and Soho made her exit.

'And then,' Winter said, looking at Angel, 'there were three . . .'

'Four,' said Twinkle indignantly. 'I can count up to six! *And* you've forgotten about—'

Winter put a finger to his lips, and Twinkle had the tact to fall silent. Pye, also tactful, made a pretence of having something to do outside, and as he left the building Winter went over to Angel and put an arm round her shoulders.

'All right?' he asked gently.

She sniffed and nodded, then found a scrap of fabric (it happened to be the torn piece of Tertia's dress, which Twinkle had brought back as a trophy) and blew her nose. 'It was just . . . her not realising that it *is* me,' she said.

'I think I understand.' Winter smiled faintly. 'Mind you, it's probably better this way. If she knew the truth, she really *would* have an Episode!'

Angel hesitated, then gave a shaky chuckle. 'And I wouldn't want to go back to Zone Celeb,' she admitted. 'Not in a million years.'

'Well, if Tertia's little band of captives were anything to go by . . . I truly think most of them thoroughly enjoyed themselves. And they've all gone back to their own realities convinced that they've taken part in the most spectacular Vee production ever made.'

She nodded. 'Pye's so clever. The way he explained it to them . . .'

'Pye's a genius. We're very lucky to be working for him.'

There was a clopping noise outside, and a large shadow fell across the door. Sometimes pushed his nose into the building and snorted, and Suuu Beeen Aaat, perched in the saddle, said, 'Goodnight, everyone! Who are you?'

'Hello, Suuu,' said Winter.

'Never—'

'Heard of her; I know, you always say that. Is Pye coming?'

'No,' said Suuu as Pye appeared. 'He isn't right behind me. Well, that was a very boring few hours, wasn't it? I liked that Tertia, but I hope she'll be discontented.'

'Yes,' Winter agreed, deciding that it wasn't worth bothering to untangle all Suuu's convolutions. 'So: who's ready to go home?'

'I'm not,' Suuu told him. 'In fact I'm staying here, and I'm not taking the horse with me. His name's Frequently, by the way.' She slid from the saddle and started to lead Sometimes towards the mirror sculpture. 'This isn't the right place to stand, is it?'

'No,' Pye assured her. 'It's completely wrong.'

'Oh, good. Or bad. Probably. Well . . . hello, then. I hope I won't see any of you again.'

Angel couldn't suppress a grin. 'Absolutely, Suuu,' she said. 'I'm sure you won't.'

Suuu smiled, then yawned. 'Okay,' she said. 'Don't operate that thing.'

It was very quiet in the building when she and Sometimes were gone. Even Twinkle was still silent. Outside, the tide had turned and was creeping in over the

179

sand. The causeway was already covered; the castle stood alone and empty on its island.

Pye had been tinkering with the mirror sculpture; at last he straightened. 'All set,' he said. 'We'll be home in time for Tee.'

'Last look at the sea?' Winter asked Angel.

She considered, then shook her head. 'No. I think I'd rather just . . . remember it.'

They all stood together in front of the sculpture. The doorway between realities opened, then closed; and the only sound that remained in the empty world was the ceaseless, surging murmur of the incoming tide.

## MIRROR MIRROR

*Part One: Breaking Through*

*Louise Cooper*

Many years into the future, in the country once known as England, Angel Ashe approaches her fifteenth birthday in Eurostate 8.

Life here holds a few surprises. Freedom of choice is a thing of the past. Falling in love is not an option. But Angel knows things could be different . . .

She has found a way to break free of her destiny and unlock the doors of time. It's easy . . . the answer lies in her own reflection.

## MIRROR MIRROR

### *Part Two: Running Free*

*Louise Cooper*

Having made it back to her own time with her new friend, Winter, Angel is forced to flee from the controlling Soho and from all the media excitement that has surrounded her disappearance.

Together Angel and Winter use the mirror sculpture to travel back to Albion. But as soon as they arrive they discover that this is not the Albion they remember – and they are not welcome. But trying to escape, to find a world they do know is more difficult than they thought – and they are faced with a terrifying situation: that they will be trapped forever in different times.

Only one person can help them make sense from their plight – but can he rescue them, before it is too late?

**THE SHAR TRILOGY**

Part One: *Daughter of Storms*

*Louise Cooper*

*The start of a compelling fantasy trilogy . . .*

Born in a supernatural storm, under a crimson sun, Shar is destined for the Sisterhood.

Innocent of the power she controls, Shar is of great value to others – who patiently lie in wait for such a soul. But as Shar begins to realise her remarkable gift, the terror begins . . .

In a land where the gods of Order and Chaos rule – a deadly power is rising. Can Shar – Daughter of Storms – summon the power and become the Dark Caller . . . ?

## THE SHAR TRILOGY

Part Two: *The Dark Caller*

*Louise Cooper*

Shar – now the Dark Caller – has a unique power: she can harness good spirits and, if she needs to, use them to destroy anyone who threatens her. So far, Shar has coped well with her growing powers – and those who defy them. But now someone wants revenge . . .

Lured into a web of terror and deceit, can Shar take on the forces that threaten her once again? And this time, will the benevolent gods be on her side?

## THE SHAR TRILOGY

Part Three: *Keepers of Light*

*Louise Cooper*

For her most dangerous challenge yet, Shar is driven to unlock the secrets of the Maze – a magical gateway through time, and a phenomenon which has long baffled the highest powers in her land.

The Maze offers Shar the power to right an old wrong, and to change the course of history – if she chooses to. But as she faces its many terrifying dimensions, will the Maze simply lead Shar into deadly temptation?

# ORDER FORM

*Louise Cooper*

| | | | |
|---|---|---|---|
| 0 340 73983 5 | RUNNING FREE | £4.99 | ❏ |
| 0 340 73982 7 | BREAKING THROUGH | £4.99 | ❏ |
| 0 340 77852 0 | DAUGHTER OF STORMS | £4.99 | ❏ |
| 0 340 77854 7 | THE DARK CALLER | £4.99 | ❏ |
| 0 340 77853 9 | KEEPERS OF LIGHT | £4.99 | ❏ |

*All Hodder Children's books are available at your local bookshop, or can be ordered direct from the publisher. Just tick the titles you would like and complete the details below. Prices and availability are subject to change without prior notice.*

Please enclose a cheque or postal order made payable to *Bookpoint Ltd*, and send to: Hodder Children's Books, 39 Milton Park, Abingdon, OXON OX14 4TD, UK.
Email Address: orders@bookpoint.co.uk

If you would prefer to pay by credit card, our call centre team would be delighted to take your order by telephone. Our direct line *01235 400414* (lines open 9.00 am–6.00 pm Monday to Saturday, 24 hour message answering service). Alternatively you can send a fax on *01235 400454*.

| TITLE | | FIRST NAME | | SURNAME | |
|---|---|---|---|---|---|

| ADDRESS | |
|---|---|
| | |
| | |
| DAYTIME TEL. | | POST CODE | |

If you would prefer to pay by credit card, please complete:
Please debit my Visa/Access/Diner's Card/American Express (delete as applicable) card no:

| | | | | | | | | | | | | | | | | | | |
|---|---|---|---|---|---|---|---|---|---|---|---|---|---|---|---|---|---|---|

Signature .......................................... Expiry Date: ....................

If you would NOT like to receive further information on our products please tick the box. ❏